"Hire her, and I'll knock off half your rent."

Bridget's eyes grew round.

"You and I have an agreement—a binding legal document—for me to rent this building. I don't want anything to complicate it."

"It wouldn't complicate anything," Mac replied.

"I'm not that naive, and neither are you."

This was not going well. Did she think he would terminate her lease if she didn't hire Kaylee?

He wasn't that kind of guy.

Bridget gazed off into the distance. "Even if I wanted an employee, I probably wouldn't hire her. If she can't be bothered to go to school, I doubt she'd come to work."

Mac prepared to defend Kaylee, but what could he say? He was new to this guardian thing. Not once had it crossed his mind that he'd have to make decisions for a minor. In his thirty-two years, he'd never fallen in love or considered marriage—and he certainly hadn't given any thought to having kids.

And here he was, responsible for his sister, clueless as to what she needed.

Jill Kemerer writes novels with love, humor and faith. Besides spoiling her mini dachshund and keeping up with her busy kids, Jill reads stacks of books, lives for her morning coffee and gushes over fluffy animals. She resides in Ohio with her husband and two children. Jill loves connecting with readers, so please visit her website, jillkemerer.com, or contact her at PO Box 2802, Whitehouse, OH 43571.

Books by Jill Kemerer

Love Inspired

Wyoming Ranchers

The Prodigal's Holiday Hope
A Cowboy to Rely On
Guarding His Secret
The Mistletoe Favor

Wyoming Sweethearts

Her Cowboy Till Christmas
The Cowboy's Secret
The Cowboy's Christmas Blessings
Hers for the Summer

Wyoming Cowboys

The Rancher's Mistletoe Bride
Reunited with the Bull Rider
Wyoming Christmas Quadruplets
His Wyoming Baby Blessing

Visit the Author Profile page at LoveInspired.com for more titles.

The Mistletoe Favor

Jill Kemerer

LOVE INSPIRED

INSPIRATIONAL ROMANCE

LOVE INSPIRED®
INSPIRATIONAL ROMANCE

PLEASE RECYCLE

Recycling programs
for this product may
not exist in your area.

ISBN-13: 978-1-335-58532-5

The Mistletoe Favor

Copyright © 2022 by Ripple Effect Press, LLC

For questions and comments about the quality of this book, please contact us
at CustomerService@Harlequin.com.

Love Inspired
22 Adelaide St. West, 41st Floor
Toronto, Ontario M5H 4E3, Canada
www.LoveInspired.com

Printed in U.S.A.

Look not every man on his own things,
but every man also on the things of others.
—*Philippians* 2:4

For Scott. My hero every Christmas.
I love our life together.

Chapter One

What was the point of being rich if he couldn't make Kaylee happy?

Mac Tolbert parked his truck on Main Street in Sunrise Bend, Wyoming. As his feet hit the pavement, he inhaled the crisp, autumn air. The downtown looked like it had been invaded by pumpkins and bales of straw. Soon they'd be replaced with Christmas lights and wreaths.

He strode toward the new storefront everyone around town was buzzing about. The window had fancy gold lettering that spelled out Brewed Awakening. After months without a coffee shop, the locals were ready for the grand opening next week. It had been a no-brainer for Mac to lease the building, including the apartment above, to Bridget Renna. Any friend of Sawyer Roth's was a friend of his, and Bridget had plenty of experience managing a coffee shop in New York City.

Although they'd only met briefly at Sawyer's wedding this summer, Mac had a favor to ask of Bridget, and he was more than willing to make it worth her while. He just prayed it would get his little sister, Kaylee, out of her funk.

"Mac! Oh, Mac!"

He turned to see who was calling his name and groaned

when he recognized Dina Jones, the president of the high school's athletic booster club, jogging toward him, waving wildly. She'd called and emailed him many times since July when his father had died in a small plane crash. It was no secret around these parts that Mac was now a multi-millionaire.

Dad had owned an energy company in Texas, in addition to multiple side businesses and properties. To say he'd been wealthy was an understatement. After his father's death, Mac had enlisted a top-notch team of lawyers to help him sell and consolidate all of the assets. Kaylee's portion had been put into a trust. The ranch had been left solely to him in the will.

Mac was still stunned at the size of the fortune his father had left behind. He didn't like to think about the fact it was now his. His relationship with his dad had been complicated.

"I'm glad I caught you." Short of breath, Dina stopped in front of him. The insurance agent was in her late forties and had two strapping boys in high school. "Have you had a chance to think about the uniforms?"

"I'm going to need more time." The words slipped off his tongue too easily. For weeks he'd been giving the same answer to everyone who approached him to donate to a worthy cause—he needed more time. Unfortunately, the more time that passed, the more frozen with indecision he became.

It wasn't that he didn't want to help them. He did. But every request made his chest feel like it was pressing through a meat grinder, and the sheer volume of petitions for aid had him longing to place a pallet of cash in the middle of town with the announcement, "Here, take it and leave me alone!"

"The booster club could really use your support," Dina

said. "Some of the football players are wearing pants two sizes too big. The elastic's worn out on others. Last week the backside of Jake Hammond's pants ripped during the game. You can imagine how embarrassed he was. Any amount you could spare would be a big help. And I hate to say it, but the bleachers have been a problem for years."

"You mentioned that." He stepped away from her. He'd heard all about the uniforms and the bleachers on more than one occasion. He didn't have time to deal with this today. "If you'll excuse me, I have an appointment."

"Oh, sure!" Dina beamed and walked in the other direction, briefly looking back to say, "You should stop by our next meeting. Think about it."

He'd think about it, all right. In a year. Two. Maybe ten. He sighed and reached for the handle of the coffee shop. Locked.

Scooting sideways to stand in front of the window, he cupped his hands to peer inside. The lights were on, and Bridget stood at the counter, unpacking a box. He watched her for a moment. Dark brown hair fell just below her shoulders. She had a straight nose, high cheekbones and thick, well-groomed eyebrows.

The woman intrigued him. Yes, her features were striking, but it was her style that caught his attention. She wore a long-sleeved, body-hugging black shirt with form-fitting gray pants and a denim apron tied around her waist. A silver necklace adorned her neck. Low-heeled black ankle boots completed the outfit.

Simple. Appealing. He couldn't take his eyes off her.

She glanced his way, and he backed up, feeling like he'd been caught spying on her. Heat rushed up his neck, but he pointed to the door, and she nodded. After she let him inside, Bridget locked the door again, then strolled to the counter and opened a cardboard box without so much as a hello.

He made his way over to the counter and took in the space, so different from the previous coffee shop. She'd painted the walls a cream color and had added pendant lighting over the counter. Strings of bare bulbs were draped across the ceiling and above the front window.

Wooden shelves lined the wall behind the counter where she'd stacked various white mugs and small plates. Glass jars full of coffee beans rested on an upper shelf. The former clunky wooden stools had been replaced by sleek metal ones, and small tables were strategically placed to create a wide aisle for people to wait in line.

It looked upscale yet comfortable. Not quite what he expected from the New York City transplant. To be honest, he wasn't sure what he'd expected.

"I paid my rent." The slightest twinkle gleamed in her dark brown eyes, as rich as the coffee beans behind her.

"I know." He pulled out a stool and sat, facing her, then looked around one more time. "I like what you've done with the place."

"Thanks." She took out a napkin dispenser from the box.

Mac wasn't sure what to say. He didn't know Bridget. Had no idea how to break the ice with her.

"You didn't stop by to sit here watching me." The nervous glance she gave him didn't match her teasing tone. "What's on your mind?"

Put like that…maybe he should just lay it out there. Mac didn't want her to be uncomfortable on his account. A prickly sensation made his arm hair stand up. He wasn't ready. "How are you settling in?"

"Fine." She set two more dispensers on the counter, lining them up, and reached into the box for another.

"If you have any problems with the apartment, call—"

"Mr. Bingham, I know." She nudged the last dispenser to be even with the others before turning her full attention to him. "His number is listed on the lease."

That it was. He clenched his jaw. Why was this so difficult? Because he rarely, if ever, asked anyone for a favor. They always asked him for them.

"Have you hired all your employees?" he asked.

"I'm a one-man band." Her white teeth flashed in a neat row as she smiled. Then she wiped her hands down her apron and narrowed her eyes slightly. "Why?"

It was as good an opening as he was going to get.

"My sister—half sister, really—Kaylee—her name is Kaylee. She's fifteen." If he could slap the nervousness out of himself, he would. "She could use a job."

Bridget didn't say a word. The way her gaze focused made him even more twitchy than he already was.

But he pressed on. "Our dad died this summer. My stepmother—Kaylee's mom—was with him in the small plane when it went down. Now Kaylee's living with me, and I don't know…the move from Texas, the loss of her parents…well, she's not doing so great."

"Define 'not doing so great.'" Her expression softened, and the small crease between her eyebrows was enough for him to keep plodding on.

"She's quiet. Not much of a social life. Misses school a lot."

"Why?"

He rubbed the back of his neck. "There are a lot of days it's too hard for her."

"You let her stay home?"

He nodded, feeling judged for some reason.

"If showing up for school's too hard for her, having a job might be, too."

She kind of had a point, but then again, she didn't understand.

"Having something besides school would be good for her. It will get her out. Force her to think about something besides…" He straightened, thumping his knuckles on the counter. "Hire her, and I'll knock off half your rent for the next six months."

Her eyes grew round. She bent to place the dispensers on shelves below the counter. Mac craned his neck to watch her.

Her face popped up. "You and I have an agreement— a binding legal document—for me to rent this building. I don't want anything to complicate it."

"It wouldn't complicate anything."

She arched her eyebrows as she straightened. "I'm not that naive, and neither are you."

Keeping his mouth shut, Mac ran his tongue over his front teeth. This was not going well. What was she getting at? Did she think he'd terminate her lease if she didn't hire Kaylee?

He wasn't that kind of guy.

He couldn't remember the last time anyone would even consider the possibility he'd do them dirty like that.

Bridget gazed off in the distance. "Even if I wanted an employee, I probably wouldn't hire her. If she can't be bothered to go to school, I doubt she'd be bothered to come to work."

Mac prepared to defend Kaylee, but what could he say? He was new to this guardian thing. Not once had it crossed his mind that he'd have to make decisions for a minor. In his thirty-two years, he'd never fallen in love or considered marriage—and he certainly hadn't given any thought to having kids.

And here he was, responsible for his sister, clueless as to what she needed.

All he knew was he loved Kaylee and would do anything to make her happy again.

"Keep your discount," Bridget said, shaking her head as if convincing herself. "I don't want it."

Bridget didn't have time for Mac's misguided attempts to help his sister. She also didn't want to spend the money to hire someone right now, although having part-time help would be necessary soon. The grand opening of Brewed Awakening was on Monday, the first of November, only four days away.

Moving to Sunrise Bend and opening a coffee shop were two dreams she couldn't quite believe were coming true. And she wanted to keep them alive as long as possible.

"You don't know Kaylee." Mac's low voice was as smooth as the Kona blend she'd made for herself in a French press this morning. "She's not spoiled. She's shy and sweet and hurting."

Shy. Sweet. Hurting.

Could have summed herself up at fifteen.

"I'm sure she's all those things, and I'm sorry you both lost your parents. Or did I get that wrong? Is your mom still alive?"

He glanced down at his hands. "My mother died when I was five. Cancer."

"Mine, too. Except it was a burst appendix when I was three."

Her gaze met his, and the understanding and compassion flowing through his gunmetal gray eyes sent shockwaves to her core. Quickly, she looked away.

The one thing she'd promised herself before stepping

foot in Sunrise Bend was to keep a low profile. She had too much riding on this move to let anything jeopardize it.

An ill-advised romance with any of the town's single ranchers would be the opposite of keeping a low profile.

She didn't know if she was capable of letting anyone get close to her, anyhow. It would mean allowing them to see the real her. Sure, she was doing fine now, but her past was embarrassing and ugly.

Thankfully, she did have one person who knew the real her. Her best friend, Sawyer Roth. For years he'd lived across the hall from her in New York City and told her tales of this town and his friends, including Mac Tolbert. And she'd hung on every word, enamored of the thought of church potlucks and miles of prairie with wild horses and looming mountains and all the other rural pleasures he talked about. Compared to the city, it had seemed so foreign, like it wasn't real.

Then, a year ago, Sawyer had moved back to Wyoming. He'd returned to ranching, fallen in love, gotten married to Tess Malone, a local rancher's daughter, and urged Bridget to come out and join him.

And so she did.

It was the scariest thing she'd ever done, and she'd had her share of scary times.

"I'm not asking for the world." Mac opened his hands to reveal his palms. She'd almost forgotten he was there. "A couple of afternoons a week. You don't even have to pay her. I will."

Like she'd ever let that happen. She let out a skeptical snort. "Look, I don't know how you do it around here, but if I'm the one benefiting from someone's work, I'm the one who pays them."

"Fine, so you'll pay her." His eyes flashed to silver as his lips kicked into a crooked grin.

"I see how you did that." Bridget wagged her finger playfully. "No. I'm not hiring her. I'm not paying her. There are lots of businesses downtown." She gestured to the door, then to the window. "Find her a job somewhere else."

He let out a pitiful sigh. "No can do."

"They won't hire her, either?" She wasn't surprised. Mac might think his sister was a ray of sunshine who could do no wrong, but she might be spoiled and using the tragedy of her parents' death to get out of going to school.

Bridget cringed. What an awful thing to assume. When had she grown so harsh?

That's not who you are, Bridge. Nip that kind of thinking in the bud right now. Keep seeing the best in people.

"I didn't say that." He glowered. "I don't want her working late. You close at five. And the coffee shop is an easy walk from the high school, at least until she gets her driver's license."

His mention of a driver's license riled up her tummy. Another thing she needed to deal with soon. If she was going to have a future in Sunrise Bend, she needed to be able to drive. She'd never be independent without her own car.

"You're not used to the word *no* are you?" She grabbed the scissors on the counter and, in one motion, sliced through the packing tape, then folded the empty box flat.

"I don't like to let people down." Sincerity radiated from him.

Bridget couldn't help studying the man. And she'd gotten an eyeful of the handsome rancher at Sawyer's wedding this summer when she'd first met him. His wide shoulders stretched under an unzipped black jacket, and a faded gray T-shirt peeked out. His cheekbones, nose and chin were chiseled perfection. The short dark brown hair and hooded gray eyes confirmed her impression that this was a man who'd been blessed.

Good looks, good friends, good life.

He was wealthy, gorgeous…and didn't even know he was acting a wee bit entitled.

He'd clearly grown up under sunshine.

She, on the other hand, had grown up under heavy storm clouds. A guy like Mac would never understand, let alone accept, a girl like her with a difficult past. He didn't need to understand, though, because she wasn't telling him.

What people didn't know they couldn't use against her.

"I meant that you don't hear the word *no* very often." She tilted her head and watched him.

"I don't ask strangers for favors very often."

"That makes two of us."

His fingers flexed. "Look, this was Sawyer's suggestion."

"Don't throw Sawyer at me." Bridget narrowed her eyes. Mac wasn't playing fair. She'd do anything for Sawyer. If it wasn't for him, she didn't know what would have become of her life.

"I didn't mean…" He had the grace to look embarrassed. Unfortunately, that made her soften to his idea. Curling her fingers into her palms, she willed her weakness away.

"Play fair or don't play at all," she said. She would not cave. She'd learned how to stand on her own two feet at a young age and expected everyone else to do the same.

"Fair? You want to talk about playing fair? My sister is lost." He stood, his expression turbulent. "She's never been a social butterfly. This move has been tough on her, and I don't know how to make it better. I'm trying. I really am. But I don't know what to do. I thought…maybe…

working here, being in town, being around another woman who's new to the area..."

Shame hit her hard. Mac was obviously worried, and all she was doing was giving him a hard time.

He was a nice man. He seemed genuine.

But he was still her landlord.

And still way too attractive. And none of this changed the fact she needed to figure out how she could fit into this town without getting hurt.

"Please?" He held her gaze, and she could hear his slow exhalation as he waited for her response.

She waffled. When Bridget was sixteen, she'd been as lost and as helpless as a person could be. And God had sent Sawyer to help her. Maybe it was time to pass on the blessing.

"Have her stop by after school tomorrow." Bridget looked down at her hands, then at him. "I'll interview her."

"Really?" His expression reminded her of the sun coming out after days of rain.

"I'm not making any promises. I'll interview her. If I think she can handle the job, I'll consider hiring her part-time. If I don't think she's up for it, I won't hire her. And I meant what I said before—no discounts on rent, and I pay her wages."

Mac thrust his right hand across the counter. "You've got it."

She shook his hand, surprised at how good his warm, strong grip felt.

"If there's anything I can do to help you..."

"Don't get ahead of yourself, cowboy." She couldn't help but smile. "I haven't hired her yet."

"Yeah, but you're giving her a chance."

A chance. Just like Sawyer had given her.

"Thanks, Bridget." Mac gave her a small wave and turned to leave. "Oh, and welcome to Sunrise Bend."

When he left, the bell above the door clanged, and she slowly walked to the door and locked it, pausing to watch him get into his truck. Then she forced herself to grab another box from the storage room.

Welcome to Sunrise Bend. If she hired Kaylee, she'd be forced to pay wages she wasn't sure she could afford. It all depended on how busy the store was. Even with no employees, her adventure in Wyoming might be short-lived. She had no idea if the town would like her coffee or if she could support herself here.

But she was willing to try.

If she kept her focus on what she knew—selling delicious coffee drinks in an inviting atmosphere—all the simple things she'd longed for when she'd listened to Sawyer's stories would be available to her, too.

This was her chance to live the life of her dreams, and she wasn't going to blow it.

"Good news," Mac announced loudly, shrugging off his jacket and hanging it on a hook in the mudroom half an hour later. He made his way to the living room.

Kaylee, wearing black leggings and an oversize red sweatshirt, sat on the sectional and flipped through channels on the television. Her light brown hair was pulled back in a messy ponytail, and she didn't bother to look up when he sat on the other end of the couch.

"Brewed Awakening is looking for part-time help." So he fibbed slightly. It was for a good cause. "The owner, Bridget Renna, wants to interview you tomorrow after school."

"Why?" She held the remote out at arm's length and gave him a sideways glance.

He hadn't thought about her questioning him. A mistake on his part.

"Well, she's new here and doesn't know many people. I told her you'd stop by."

She let out a long, slow sigh and let the remote fall on her lap. "I don't feel good."

Tension tightened his neck. Kaylee hadn't been feeling good since the moment she'd moved in with him back in July. He'd been patient with her. He still was. But his patience was wearing thin.

"The interview won't take long."

She ignored him. "If my head hurts, I'm not going to school."

"You can take a Tylenol." He usually didn't push back about her lingering headaches and stomachaches, but something had shifted inside him since asking Bridget to hire her. The doctors couldn't find anything wrong with Kaylee. They'd chalked it up to stress. "Lots of people make it through work or school with a headache."

"What if my stomach gets upset?" She faced him, her expression full of worry.

"What if it doesn't?"

"Don't joke." Her hazel eyes closed briefly. "I'm serious, Mac."

He reached over and covered her hand with his own. "I am, too. But you can't miss any more school, Kay. I know sophomore year hasn't been all it's cracked up to be."

Her shoulders slumped so much he was afraid her head would disappear into her neck like a turtle.

"I don't know how to make coffee." Those blinking eyes, full of insecurity, made his muscles tense.

"She'll train you. And this is just an interview. She might not hire you." Maybe he was pushing Kaylee too hard. It wasn't as if Bridget even wanted to hire her. He *could* call the interview off.

Kaylee pressed the heel of her hand into her left temple. "Is she one of those rah-rah people? Like Mrs. Duvern? I can't work for someone who expects me to smile constantly."

"She's not a rah-rah person. Bridget's from New York City, and I think she would want you to be yourself." But would she? Maybe he was wrong about that, too. What if Bridget hired Kaylee and put all kinds of unreasonable demands on her? Like smiling constantly?

Come on. Smiling at customers was not an unreasonable demand.

"New York City?" She brightened. "Mom and I went there last year." It had been so long since he'd seen Kaylee look anything but insecure and miserable, he'd forgotten how pretty and full of life his sister could be. "We shopped at all these cool stores and went to museums and the Statue of Liberty. She said we would do all the touristy stuff since it was my first time."

"I've never been there, myself." He had no desire to go, either. He'd spent a good portion of his childhood being left in hotels with a nanny in various cities whenever Dad went on business trips. He couldn't remember going to New York, though. As he'd grown older, he'd resented being taken out of school for his dad's whims, especially since his father never spent any time with him on those trips.

Always closing a deal. That summed up his dad.

It was Kaylee's turn to cover his hand. "Someday we'll go, and I'll show you around."

"I'd like that." For Kaylee he'd visit New York City, even if he didn't really want to.

An easy silence stretched.

"Should I walk over there after school?" Frowning, she rubbed her lips together.

"I'll pick you up and take you."

"What should I wear?"

"What do you want to wear?" Over the past months, Mac had learned that giving advice about clothes was a no-win situation.

"I don't know." She looked down at her leggings. "This outfit is comfortable."

Comfortable? It was one step above pajamas in his opinion.

"What about those jeans you wore a few weeks ago?" As soon as the words were out, he fought the urge to clap his hand over his mouth. Why had he said anything? He knew better than to break his rule about clothing advice. He braced himself for the worst.

"Those jeans don't fit right." She wrapped her arms around her waist, hugging herself tightly.

And this was why he avoided talking about clothes. "They look good on you."

"No, they don't." Her face pinched.

He didn't know what to say. Kaylee couldn't wear athletic clothing to the interview. He doubted Bridget would find it inspiring, and he'd already overstepped every boundary with the woman by asking her to take a chance on his sister. If Kaylee didn't make a good impression, Bridget wouldn't hire her.

And he really wouldn't blame her.

"Hey, just wear something you wouldn't wear to bed or to exercise in. Jeans and a sweater. Easy."

She covered her face with her hands. "But what jeans? What sweater?"

He almost mentioned phoning a friend, but the one and only time he'd said those words, she'd burst into tears and told him they'd think she was weird. From his memories of high school, girls always talked on the phone about what they were wearing. Maybe things had changed since then.

"I'm calling Lydia." Kaylee stood. "She probably knows what I should wear."

"Yes, call Lydia," he said, keeping his tone light. Lydia. Hmm…had she made a friend, finally? This was news to celebrate.

"If I don't have anything to wear, you'll have to tell the New York lady I won't be there."

Wasn't happening. Kaylee would be there if it meant he had to buy her a new outfit himself.

Yeah, she'd be there.

He'd had to go way outside of his comfort zone to even ask Bridget for this favor. There was something about the woman that simultaneously drew him while intimidating him.

She seemed comfortable in her own skin. But guarded. She definitely didn't want anything from him. Unlike most people around here.

Did Bridget see right through the wealthy-rancher, nice-guy persona everyone else in Sunrise Bend seemed to accept? Or did she see the side of him his father had disapproved of?

He lurched to his feet. He needed to set the table.

It didn't really matter how Bridget viewed him. He just hoped his instincts were correct that an after-school job would help bust Kaylee out of her shell. He didn't want her to have any more pain. The kid had had enough for a lifetime.

Chapter Two

After spending her entire life in New York City, Bridget was starting to have serious doubts she was cut out for rural living. Later that afternoon Bridget browsed the selections at the local hardware store and realized how limited her shopping options were. In the city, she could walk, take a bus, ride the subway or use a car service or rideshare app to get anywhere. She'd loved the variety of restaurants and stores. Taken it for granted, really.

Sunrise Bend didn't even have a Walmart or Target. Nor was there a furniture or home goods store.

She needed lamps for the living room and a fluffy rug to chase away the chill from the hardwood floors. If only she had a car…

And a driver's license.

Her nerves crackled at the thought. She'd have to learn how to drive if she was going to get a driver's license. And she needed a vehicle to have any kind of future here. She couldn't expect Sawyer to drive her all the time.

A license was crucial to her new life…but someone would have to teach her how to drive first.

One problem at a time.

Bridget shuffled farther down the aisle, barely noticing

the lightbulbs and boxes of overhead light fixtures. Her huge yawn took her by surprise, although it shouldn't have. She'd yet to get more than three hours of uninterrupted sleep, and she'd been living here for almost two weeks.

Sunrise Bend was quiet. Too quiet. And the noises she did hear at night freaked her out. Blustery winds, animals howling in the distance—coyotes? Wolves? Owls? Wait, owls hooted, didn't they? She had no idea, but she'd take sirens, horns, garbage trucks and people yelling at each other over those any day. The white-noise app on her phone wasn't helping, either.

Thankfully, she'd been so busy getting the coffee shop ready that her lack of sleep had been the least of her worries. But now that the shop was almost finished, she needed to get more shut-eye. Making her apartment cozy could only help.

She meandered down to the end of the aisle. She'd either have to make do with what Sunrise Bend offered, which at the moment seemed to be a selection of three ugly lamps, or order everything online.

Grimacing, she checked the price tags. At least they were in her price range.

Sawyer would take her to the nearest town if she asked him, but she didn't want to drag him away from Tess. As much as they tried to deny it, they were still in their newlywed phase. She wouldn't disrupt their happiness.

Besides, if she went to a supercenter, she'd end up spending more than she could afford, and she needed to track every penny until she knew where she stood financially with the coffee shop.

It had to be successful.

If it wasn't? She didn't know what she'd do. Go back to New York most likely, but even with the lack of shopping options and eerie silence, she preferred to stay here in Wyoming.

Voices carried from the next aisle over. "I don't see what all the fuss is about. If Riley couldn't keep the coffee shop going, no one can. Betsy told me she went to Denver this summer, and they charged seven bucks for a cup of coffee there. If some city girl thinks I'm going to pay seven dollars for a cup of coffee, she can think again…"

Bridget froze. She couldn't make out the garbled response, but she guessed it was from another woman.

"Why does she want to move out to the sticks, anyway?" The first woman spoke again. "Running from something probably. Or someone."

"True." A phlegmy cough followed.

"Six months. I give it six months before the coffee shop shuts down for good."

"Marge and Bud made a go of it all those years." The cough persisted. "Riley didn't exactly have the best business sense—"

"Six months." The voices faded as they moved on.

Bridget's heartbeat pounded. She had to get out of there. With long strides, she marched all the way down the aisle and out the door. When she made it to the sidewalk, she took a deep breath. Six months, huh? They were probably right.

It wasn't as if she had a business degree. She didn't even have a high school diploma. With Sawyer's help, she'd at least gotten her GED.

Could she really succeed here? Sure, she'd *managed* coffee shops, but owning one was a whole different animal.

Bridget pulled her shoulders back and forced her feet forward.

Who cared what those ladies thought? She was going to make this shop succeed. And, no, she wasn't going to charge seven dollars for a cup of coffee. She was charging a fair market price.

Walking in the direction of her apartment, she mentally reviewed the prices she'd decided on. Were they too high?

She whipped out the phone from her cross-body purse and called Sawyer. After two rings, he answered. "What's up?"

"How much is too much to charge for a coffee around here?"

"Um…where is this coming from?"

"Just wondering." She accelerated to a power walk, missing the sounds of traffic and sirens, missing the crush of people on the sidewalk, missing the unique stores to dip into and lose herself for an hour or two.

Out in the Wyoming air, she felt open, exposed, all by herself.

"You okay?" he asked.

"I'm merely having a pre-opening freak-out."

"The prices we went over sounded reasonable to me. And Tess knows a lot about it. She thought you were spot-on."

Gratitude made her throat tighten. Why was she questioning herself?

Because this was *her* business.

She no longer had a boss. She was the boss. And it scared her.

"Thanks, Sawyer. I needed to hear that."

"Want me to pick you up? You can have supper with us, and we'll hash it out again."

Nothing sounded better than a meal with Sawyer, Tess, her father Ken, and her little boy Tucker. But they'd had her over twice already. She wouldn't wear out her welcome.

"No, I'm working on the apartment tonight."

"Need me to drive you anywhere for supplies?"

Of course, he would offer. Her tension eased at his thoughtfulness.

"I'll be all right," she said. "I'll let you go. Tell Tess hi for me."

"Hey, Bridget?"

"Yeah?" She strode past the park with the lovely white gazebo she'd gravitated to on more than one occasion, then checked both ways before crossing the street.

"We're here for you. Whatever you need. Okay?"

"Thanks." She told him goodbye and ended the call.

What she needed was some time to get her head on straight. Her cluttered, unpacked apartment wasn't a good place for that.

She backtracked to the park. As she strolled, she burrowed her hands into her coat pockets. The weather had a bite to it, something she was used to from cold winters in the city. Dead brown leaves blew past her, tumbling in a race to some unknown destination.

When she reached the gazebo, she paused to take it in. With hay bales, pumpkins and mums at the entrance, it looked like a photo spread in a country magazine. She went inside and sat on one of the benches.

She took the opportunity to pray. *God, I've pushed away my doubts about opening Brewed Awakening, and I've ignored all the worries about people rejecting me. But they're back. I mean, I know who I am. I know who I'm not. I just want people to have a place to relax with a good cup of coffee. And I want to enjoy the simple pleasures of small-town living and celebrate Christmas—really celebrate it—for once.*

She never could have afforded her own shop in the city. That was one of the highlights of moving here—the unbelievably inexpensive lease. No more dealing with her employer's bad moods or being at the mercy of a schedule she had little control over.

Here, she was in charge.

Plus, the apartment above the coffee shop was the largest she'd ever rented. It had two bedrooms, a full kitchen, a spacious living room overlooking Main Street and even a washer and dryer. She loved it.

Getting to her feet, she hugged her coat more tightly to her body. As she followed the lane to the sidewalk, her mind drifted to what Mac had told her about his sister earlier. Bridget didn't want to sympathize, but how could she not?

Kaylee had lost her parents in a terrible accident. Her world had turned upside down. Bridget could relate.

At least Mac wanted his sister to be happy. He was providing for her. Caring for her. It was more than her own "family" had done. She doubted she'd ever see her stepmother or stepsister again, and it was fine with her.

Yes, she'd give Kaylee the benefit of the doubt tomorrow. But if the girl seemed entitled or spoiled, Bridget wouldn't hire her.

There were no free rides in life. Her stepmother had drilled that into her head and had made sure Bridget learned it the hard way.

The following afternoon, Mac drummed his fingertips against the steering wheel of the truck as he waited in the parking lot of the high school for Kaylee to come out. She'd spent over an hour on the phone last night with Lydia—a girl from church in the same biology class as her—before settling on dark jeans and a burgundy sweater. He wasn't sure what brought him more relief—the fact she had a friend or that she was dressed appropriately for the interview.

His cell phone rang. He glanced at the school doors. No sign of school letting out yet. He answered the call. "Mac speaking."

"Hi, Mac, it's John Lutz."

"How's Mary doing?" Mac had a soft spot for the elderly couple. Mary had been dropping off homemade cinnamon rolls to him every Easter and Christmas ever since he hired their grandson as a ranch hand years ago. John also helped him and the rest of the crew with branding calves whenever they needed him. They were fine people.

"She's good. Getting around on the new hip just fine."

"Glad to hear it. What can I do for you?"

"The conservation district members had our monthly meeting last night. A while back we applied for a grant to repair the irrigation diversion from Crystal Creek. It's the one that washed out two years ago."

"I remember."

"I figured you would. Well, long story short, we didn't get the money. So now we've got three options—put another tax levy on the ballot, privately fund the project or leave it unrepaired. We all know how another tax levy would go over around here. Forget it. And leaving it unrepaired hurts the crops and the cattle."

Mac could see where this was going. He understood their dilemma, and he didn't blame John for calling, but his stomach tightened anyway.

John cleared his throat. "We voted to try to privately fund it, and we're asking you for help."

"I'll have to think about it." A sour taste sprouted as the words left his mouth. How many times had he said them in the past three months? And how much time had he actually spent thinking about it—any of it? The requests for donations had been coming in hot and didn't seem to be cooling at this point.

"Take your time. I'll get a detailed list of the estimates to you. Thank you, Mac."

After saying goodbye, Mac hung up and tucked away the request to consider later.

Much later.

Right now he had enough to think about. He'd decided to try a different approach with the cattle this year. Last week, he'd sold half the weaned calves, and he was keeping the other half to sell at a higher weight in the spring. It was an experiment he'd long considered doing, and he figured the time was right with the price of grain being low.

It was more than the price of grain being low, though. This was the first year he didn't have to worry about his dad threatening to sell the ranch if Mac didn't do things his way. Keeping some of the calves would mean he'd need to make sure he had enough food for them all and watch them closely this winter to make sure they were gaining enough weight.

Watching cattle was his main job in life. It came naturally to him.

But he had other jobs, other responsibilities now, too. And it all felt overwhelming.

The fact his dad was gone…

Mac clenched his jaw. He wouldn't think about it. There had been so much left unsaid between them.

His dad had thought keeping half the calves would be stupid. Was it stupid?

A stream of students poured out of the school. A few minutes later the passenger door opened, and Kaylee, looking flushed and panicky, climbed inside the truck.

"How was school?" He started the engine. She shook her head slightly as if too traumatized to speak. Anxiety gripped him. "What? What happened?"

"I hate it here," she whispered, staring off to the side.

And there it was. The declaration he'd dreaded hearing since finding out he was responsible for Kaylee. Mac had known he was inadequate as a parent figure. He'd also known ripping his sister from her prep school near Dallas would be hard on her. He'd just never imagined how hard.

"I'm sorry, Kay." He swallowed to ease the guilt lodged in his throat. "If you want, you can go home and skip the interview. I don't know what happened at school, but—"

"No!" She flashed him a wide-eyed glare. "I'm going to the interview."

"Are you sure?" He didn't see why she'd want to if her day had been so miserable. He checked for traffic and backed out of the parking spot. "Want to tell me what happened?"

She shook her head. "It doesn't matter."

It did matter. Or she wouldn't be so upset.

Maybe keeping her here in Sunrise Bend was wrong.

"Look, I've been thinking about it." Mac glanced her way as they waited in the line of traffic. "Maybe you need a trip back to Dallas to see your friends. I can take you there for a few days if you want." He inched the truck forward.

"No, Mac." She looked straight ahead, her French braid showing signs of unraveling along the sides of her face. "There's nothing left for me there."

He wouldn't be surprised if she said there was nothing left for her anywhere. The traffic started moving, and he turned onto Main Street.

"If you change your mind…"

The coffee shop was only a few blocks away. She shrank into herself and didn't say a word. He slid the truck into an open spot in front of the shop.

"Want me to wait out here?" he asked.

With her lips drawn together tightly, she nodded. Then she climbed out, shut the door and didn't look back. Once she was safely inside, Mac cut the engine and rubbed his jaw.

If he thought it would make her happy, he'd offer to move back to Dallas until she graduated from high school. Leaving the ranch would about kill him, but for Kaylee, he would put his life on hold for a few years. Thankfully, she didn't seem to want to return to Texas. The relief at the thought shamed him, but the fact remained he was glad he wouldn't have to make that particular sacrifice.

Sunrise Bend was home. The one place he'd ever felt like he could be himself.

Well, that wasn't entirely true. He might be popular around town, but it didn't mean he was an open book when it came to the personal stuff.

Sometimes he felt like God was the only One who saw right through to the real him.

His friends had his back—that was for sure. But even they didn't know how conflicted he felt about his larger-than-life father. Or his larger-than-life inheritance.

Maybe Kaylee was conflicted, too. At this point, he had no idea what his sister needed, and he didn't know if working with Bridget would help or hurt her.

He'd give this interview five minutes. Tops. His sister definitely wasn't the bubbly, customer-friendly employee a coffee shop needed. He doubted Bridget would hire her.

He never should have meddled.

Bridget had nervous flutters in her stomach when Kaylee entered the shop. She'd done the math, and she might be able to hire the girl a few days a week. But it would be a sticky situation with Mac being the landlord and all. What if Bridget had to fire his sister for some reason? Would Mac be vindictive? Make life hard for her in Sunrise Bend?

She wouldn't be able to blend in or disappear into the crowd the way she had in the city. There was no crowd here to blend in with.

Kaylee approached the counter with a pinched expression on her delicate face. She was skinny with long, loosely braided, light brown hair. She had big hazel eyes and an air of fragility about her. Bridget was glad to see she wore jeans and a sweater instead of the casual leggings and athletic wear so common among high school kids.

"You must be Kaylee." Bridget gave her a warm smile and waved her to a table. "Have a seat."

The teen looked at her shyly and sat in one of the chairs. Bridget had done her share of hiring over the past few years, and the girl's obvious discomfort had her mentally tossing out her typical interview questions. She'd set her at ease as best as she could before getting to the interview.

"Want a latte? A frap?" Bridget jerked her thumb over her shoulder.

"No, thank you." The slight longing in her expression belied her words, though.

"Well, I need a caffeine fix, so tell me about yourself while I make myself one." She went behind the counter and began making two vanilla lattes. If Kaylee declined to drink it, no harm done. Bridget could always drink it herself. Who cared about being kept up at night from the caffeine? It wasn't as if she was getting any sleep, anyhow.

"What do you want to know?" Kaylee blinked those big eyes and gripped her hands tightly together.

"How old are you?"

"Fifteen. Almost sixteen," she added quickly. "My birthday's in January."

"Really? Mine, too. What day is yours?" She pumped vanilla syrup into the mugs and started steaming the milk.

"The twenty-third."

"No. Way." Bridget whirled to face her. "That's my birthday, too."

Happiness blossomed on the girl's face, and Bridget realized how pretty she was. Mac was right about her being shy. Not the easiest personality trait to have when trying to get through the awkward teen years.

"When did you move here?" Bridget poured the first espresso, topped it with the steamed milk and made a puppy face design in it. Then she repeated the process and brought both over to the table, setting one in front of Kaylee.

"July." The frown appeared again.

"I'm sorry about your parents." She took a seat and held the cup between her hands. "I lost my dad when I was in junior high. My mom died when I was really young."

Kaylee blinked curiously at her.

"How are you settling in?"

The girl lifted one shoulder in a shrug and turned her attention to the latte. "Hey, it's a puppy. How did you do that?"

"It's easy once you know how." Bridget took a sip, lingering over the rich flavor. "A little trick I picked up back home."

"You're from New York City, right? My mom took me there last summer." Her gaze sparked with a touch of admiration.

"I lived there my entire life."

Kaylee looked around the shop. "I like how you decorated this with the lights and everything. It's chill."

"Thank you." Bridget suppressed a smile. *Chill.* Spoken like a true teenager. "I heard it had an abundance of red plaid and stuffed moose before it closed."

"Yeah, it did." The girl pulled a face. "This is much better. Did you have a coffee shop like this in New York?"

"No, I worked at a similar one, though."

"Why did you want to move here?" The question wasn't snotty, merely curious. Kaylee sipped the latte and seemed to like it.

Bridget took another drink before answering. "I didn't fit there anymore. I thought I might fit here."

"Really? You?" She blinked before her expression grew sad. "I don't fit anywhere."

Their gazes met, and Bridget knew deep down she'd raid her savings if necessary to hire this girl.

The raw ache of her own life at sixteen had dulled over the years, but it was always there under layers of emotional scar tissue.

"I guess that makes two of us," Bridget said softly.

"Not you. You're…" Kaylee flushed.

"What?" She tilted her head, interested to hear her reasoning.

"Sophisticated." She averted her gaze. "Like, look at your outfit."

Bridget looked down, not seeing anything special about it. She'd been wearing the same uniform to work for years—leotard-style long-sleeve black T-shirt, slim-fitting black or gray pants, denim apron and either black boots or ballet flats.

"I'm not a real clothes person." Bridget brushed a piece of lint off her sleeve. "This outfit is easy."

"Nothing about clothes is easy for me." The girl continued drinking her latte.

"No? I like your outfit. It looks good on you. But hey, we all have our struggles. Getting used to the quiet here isn't easy for me." She traced the rim of her mug. "I've been here for two weeks and still can't sleep."

"What do you mean?"

"It's so eerie at night." She looked off into the distance. "I'm used to city noises, not wind and wild animals."

"I never thought about it. I visited Mac for a few weeks every summer before moving here, so maybe I'm used to it."

"You did?" It surprised her. She wouldn't have thought his ranch had much to offer a young girl.

"Yeah. I actually like how peaceful it is here." Her voice grew stronger. "When I wake up, I go out to the stables and sneak carrots to the horses."

"I've never touched a horse." A small shiver rippled down her back.

"You should come over. Mac has lots of them."

"Do you ride?"

"Yeah, it's fun. I could show you how." Her bright eyes lost a bit of their shimmer. "That is, if you want to."

She didn't want to, but she didn't have the heart to hurt the girl's feelings.

"Well, if I'm going to live in Wyoming, I should probably learn how to ride a horse. But I'll wait until next summer when it's warm." If she made it here that long. What kind of thinking was that? She could not afford to indulge in negative self-talk. It would do her no good.

Brewed Awakening would succeed. Period.

"Okay, be honest," Bridget asked. "Did Mac force you to come today?"

Pink stained her cheeks. "Kind of."

"Well, he asked me to interview you. I told him I would only hire you if I thought you'd make a good employee."

Her face fell.

"He told me you miss school sometimes."

Kaylee glanced away, not responding.

"If you're going to work for me, you have to show up for every shift. I need someone I can rely on."

Her gaze darted to Bridget's. "Does this mean you're hiring me?"

"That's up to you. Can I trust you to show up?"

She nodded, a hint of awe in her expression.

"You have to go to school, too. It's important to get your high school diploma. Your mom...she'd want you to do well. No skipping."

"I know." Kaylee traced a figure eight on the table. "It's just hard sometimes."

"Life is hard." Bridget wanted to give her a hug, but a sympathetic tilt of the head would have to do.

"Not for everyone."

Truer words had not been spoken.

"You're right," Bridget said. "It doesn't change your situation, though. Regardless of what other people's lives are like, you only have yours, and you have to make the most of it."

"You wouldn't understand…"

"I would, and I do." She debated how much to tell her. "I lost everything when I was sixteen."

Kaylee stared at her with questions in her eyes.

"I survived. You will, too." And that was all she was willing to say on the subject. "Do you think you could work after school for a couple of hours during the week?"

"Yes." She nodded eagerly. "You close at five, right?"

"I do."

"Then I'll work every day after school."

"Not every day." Bridget didn't want to give her the impression she expected her to work all the time. "I know you have homework and other obligations. How about Mondays and Wednesdays for now?"

"Okay." She drew in a deep breath and straightened her shoulders. "Don't worry, I'll show up. And I won't skip school, either."

Bridget stood and held out her hand. Kaylee rose, too, and shook it.

"What should I call you?" the girl asked.

"Call me Bridget. I'll start training you on Monday."

Chapter Three

Mac did a double take when he saw Kaylee practically skipping to the truck. She looked impossibly young and full of joy. The way she used to be. Relief tumbled through him. Maybe he wasn't the worst guardian in the world.

"How did it go?" He didn't need to ask, but he did anyway as she climbed into the passenger seat.

"Great!" She beamed. "I start on Monday."

"That *is* great." He backed out of the spot and headed home. Bridget had actually hired her. He'd been certain she wouldn't. "You must have impressed her."

"She told me I have to show up to every shift, and I can't miss school."

He had to hand it to Bridget—the school condition was smart thinking.

"She made puppy faces in our lattes." Kaylee pulled the seat belt across her chest and buckled it. "She's going to teach me how, too…"

Mac started driving home. As she chattered about how *chill* the coffee shop was, his chest swelled. Finally. She was acting like a normal, lively teenager. All due to Bridget.

"Did you know she's never touched a horse?" Kaylee asked. "I told her she has to come out to the ranch sometime, but she said she wanted to wait until it's warm, like next summer…"

His spirits dampened as he turned onto the country road leading to the ranch. He wanted Kaylee to have a reason to get out of the house. To be around other people. But he sensed a bit of hero worship in the air. He didn't want her thinking she was going to be best friends with Bridget. The woman was a good ten years older than Kaylee. Was he setting up his sister for another painful letdown?

"And she and I have the same birthday. Can you believe it?"

"That's great." He would not pop her cheerful mood.

She continued to chatter, and he listened with half an ear as he watched the prairie rolling by. At least it was Friday. He'd invited his friends and their significant others over tonight. He'd made a couple batches of chili and put them in slow cookers earlier, and everyone else was bringing a side dish. It might be smart to have Kaylee invite Lydia over, too.

"Did you want to have any of your friends over tonight? The guys are coming. Tess, Holly and Hannah, too."

"You should invite Bridget." Her eyes glowed with expectation.

"I, uh, I'm sure she's busy." He didn't know why he felt hesitant. Maybe because he viewed Bridget differently than the other women around here. Which meant he was noticing her. And he didn't want to notice her.

"She's not busy." Kaylee rolled her eyes. "She doesn't have any friends here, Mac."

"That's not true," he snapped. "Sawyer is her friend."

"Right, and you said Sawyer and Tess are coming."

He pressed his lips together and kept his eyes on the road. Kaylee had gone from quiet and withdrawn to very opinionated in a split second.

"She'll feel left out if you don't invite her." Couldn't she let the topic drop?

"I'll invite her." His gut tightened at the thought. "But you should invite one of your friends over, too."

He sensed her shrinking in the passenger seat. "They all have plans."

"Like what?"

"The away football game. They were all talking about it when school let out."

He cringed. He probably should have known there was an away game and offered to take her to it. "Do you want to go?"

"No." The word was firm. "I'd have no one to sit with."

"Is Lydia going?"

She shrugged.

He debated his next move. "I'll ask Bridget to come over if you ask Lydia."

She sighed. "Whatever."

And just like that, they were back to pre-interview Kaylee. He couldn't keep up with the change in moods. He longed to saddle his horse and check cattle for eighteen hours. Anything to avoid this pervasive feeling of failing at parenting. Every. Single. Day.

They rode the rest of the way home in silence, and Kaylee went straight to her room as soon as they arrived. He took out his phone and stared at it for a few minutes.

Why was he hesitating? He'd adopted a more-the-merrier attitude from the day he moved to the ranch years ago. Otis Hanson had been running the place, and he and his wife, Helen, had encouraged him to have friends over on weekends. In many ways, Otis and Helen had been the parents he'd needed. Helen had died ten years ago. And Otis, in his seventies now, still came out to the ranch for a few hours most days.

Mac appreciated the friendships he'd developed with

his best friends—Sawyer Roth, Austin Watkins and his brother Randy, Jet Mayer and his brother Blaine—more than ever.

Until recently, they'd all been single with no plans to change. Then Sawyer had gotten married, Jet had asked Holly to marry him and Randy had proposed to Hannah. The single guys were dropping like the thermometer in January—hard and fast. So far, only he, Austin and Blaine remained free from romantic entanglements. He wanted to keep it that way.

Although with Austin being a single father, that would likely change down the line. Austin had never given them an explanation for baby AJ showing up in his life, and the guys hadn't asked. His love life was none of their business.

Mac's wasn't anyone's business, either.

But he'd promised Kaylee to invite Bridget tonight, and he kept his promises. He swiped to find her contact information.

Echoes of his father's lectures sounded in his head. He'd shoved them down many times. The first one regarding women had been shortly before he moved here. He'd been fourteen, sitting in front of Dad's massive desk as his father leaned back, toying with a pen, and gave him the squinty once-over that always made him feel no more than two inches tall.

They hadn't even been talking about girls. In fact, Mac had gone into his father's home office to ask if he could move to Sunrise Bend permanently. He wanted to work the cattle with Otis and go to high school with his new friends. He was tired of being left with housekeepers while his dad traveled constantly, and he hated his school. The ranch had felt like home.

Dad had bellowed about going to prep school and getting an MBA, but Mac, for once, had held firm and stood up for himself. The longer his father stared at him, the more he felt his dream of ranching slipping away. Then his father had leaned forward with a glint in his eye and said, "Maybe it's better this way. Hard work will do you some good. But never forget you've got money and everyone in Sunrise Bend knows it. Women are going to walk all over you, boy."

A blast of music coming from Kaylee's room made him blink.

In the following years, Dad came out to visit occasionally, making it clear that he owned the ranch and could do anything he wanted with the property, like building luxury cabins for his rich buddies to come stay in while hunting. Never consulted Mac about them. Or designing a pole barn purely for entertaining purposes although Mac had no use for it. Or sending an interior designer and construction crew to completely renovate the house with no input from Mac.

His father had never consulted him about his plans. Mac had always been at the man's mercy. He couldn't remember a time when his father hadn't threatened to sell the ranch if Mac didn't fall into line with what he wanted. And he couldn't remember a time when his dad had ever thought him capable of having a real relationship with a woman. The word *prenup* had been thrown around too many times to count.

Which, now that Mac thought about it, was probably the reason he hadn't had a serious girlfriend in a decade. He'd never allowed himself to get too close to anyone.

The ranch meant too much to him. And getting lectured about prenups and being threatened with losing this place had done their job.

"Did you ask Bridget?" Kaylee called from the hallway.

No. He didn't want to invite her over.

"Calling her now." He grimaced at his phone.

His father was dead. The ranch was Mac's. No one

could take it away from him. But the words lingered. *Women are going to walk all over you, boy.*

He pressed Bridget's number. He'd managed to keep his heart safe for thirty-two years. He could keep it safe for one measly Friday get-together.

"Hello?"

"Hey, Bridget," he said, feeling like a crackling-voiced teen. "I'm having friends over tonight for chili. You're welcome to join us. You met them all at Sawyer's wedding."

"Oh, thank you." She didn't sound thankful or excited. "Um, I'll have to pass."

Relief poured in, followed closely by regret. "Next time, then."

"Sure."

"Thank you for hiring Kaylee."

"You're welcome."

She wasn't much of a talker—that was for sure. "I guess I'll see you around."

"Yes. Thanks again for the invite." And she ended the call.

He frowned at the screen as a swirl of impressions hit him. She hadn't been happy he called. Didn't want to spend time with him or his friends. And had given him a limp thank-you for the invitation.

Huh.

What had he expected? For her to jump at the chance to come over?

Shoving the phone in his pocket, he realized that yeah, he had kind of thought she would jump at the chance. Most of the single women around here would have.

He cringed. Boy, that sounded conceited.

Kaylee padded out to the living room. "Well?"

"She can't make it."

Her face fell. "Lydia's on her way to the game."

Mac put his arm around her shoulders. "Guess it's just me and you and the rest of the gang."

She slid her arm around his waist and gave it a squeeze. "At least you tried."

Did she think he was heartbroken Bridget wasn't coming over? He wasn't. "We both tried. Next time we should plan something in advance."

"Yeah." Her eyes brightened. "When I start working next week, I'll ask Bridget to come over next Friday."

He'd meant Lydia, but he wouldn't rain on Kaylee's sunny mood. The novelty of Bridget might wear off once Kaylee was actually around her, working for her. And if it didn't? At least she had something to look forward to, someone to admire.

He just wished it wasn't Bridget. Because he suspected he was as drawn to her as Kaylee was, and he didn't like it.

The grand opening was going better than she'd dared to hope. Bridget wiped down the counter during a lull on Monday afternoon. Sawyer and his friends had all stopped by in the morning. The guys had ordered plain coffees while the ladies had selected specialty drinks. The fact they'd all shown up to support her had made her a bit teary-eyed, and she normally wasn't a crier.

Sawyer being one of her first customers wasn't a surprise, but his friends? Their support had been unexpected. It touched her.

A steady stream of customers had come in all day until about an hour ago, when it slowed. She'd fielded a lot of questions. Some personal, some general. She'd truthfully answered the general questions and deflected the personal ones as best as she could.

Only a few people had commented about Riley Sampson running the shop before her, and Bridget had listened politely, ignoring the clear implication that if Riley hadn't been able to make the coffee shop succeed, Bridget had no chance, either. They were wrong.

That being said, she would be the first to admit it had been challenging taking the orders and making all the drinks by herself. Kaylee was set to arrive any minute. Bridget craned her neck to see out the window.

If she showed up…

That wasn't fair. Just because Mac had said she'd been missing school didn't mean Bridget couldn't trust her. As if on cue, the bell above the door clanged, and Kaylee hurried inside, a backpack hanging by one strap off her shoulder.

"Hi, I got here as soon as I could."

"Come on back." Bridget's chest heaved in relief as she waved her to the doorway leading to the back room. She'd taken a risk in hiring Kaylee, and she wanted it to work out. Bridget showed her where to put her backpack and handed her a denim apron identical to her own. "Okay, if you're ready, I'll show you the ropes."

They returned to the counter, and Bridget began explaining the coffee drinks and where everything was located. The bell clanged again, and a group of teens entered, laughing and roughhousing. Bridget went to the register to take their orders while Kaylee hung back.

"Hey, Kaylee, I didn't know you worked here." An athletic-looking boy Bridget guessed to be around sixteen grinned at the girl.

"Today's my first day," she said quietly. Her cheeks were rosy, and she looked like she wished the earth would swallow her whole. Bridget knew that feeling well.

"Move it, Tanner." A striking brunette girl with expertly applied makeup playfully shoved his arm. "Some of us are ready to order."

Bridget was used to teen banter, so she waited patiently for them to settle down.

"I'll have the cinnamon-roll latte," the brunette said. "Oh, wait, salted caramel sounds good, too. Which one's better?"

"They're both delicious," Bridget assured her. "I drizzle icing on the cinnamon-roll latte, though. Gives it an extra sugar kick."

"Ooh, I'll take that." Her eyes sparkled as she paid and moved to the end of the counter, joking with one of the guys along the way.

Bridget beckoned Kaylee over and showed her how to use the cash register as they took the other three orders. Then Bridget began making the drinks, carefully explaining the steps to make each one. Kaylee didn't say much, just nodded with a terrified look in her eyes.

As the drinks were finished, Bridget called each name and noted how Tanner's gaze followed Kaylee when he came up for his. The other three teased each other and oohed and aahed over the designs Bridget had made in their foam. "Look, a pumpkin!" and "I got a fox because I *am* a fox." Groans filled the air.

She started reviewing the different drinks with Kaylee and couldn't help noticing the girl's distraction as she kept peeking over to the table of teens every few minutes. Bridget didn't blame her—there had been times when she'd struggled to concentrate when a cute guy was around, too.

Admittedly, cute guys still tended to distract her.

Mac came to mind. He was easy on the eyes, all right. When he'd called to invite her over last Friday, she'd almost yelled yes, but caution held her back. She was already too involved with her landlord now that she'd hired Kaylee, and if she wasn't careful, she could jeopardize her business, not to mention her heart.

"Don't worry about remembering everything." Bridget steepled her fingers. "I'll type up instructions on how to make all the drinks." She glanced at the group. "Do you go to school with them?"

"Yeah. They're juniors. Older."

"You're a sophomore, right?"

She nodded.

"Tanner seems to like you."

Her eyes grew round and she shook her head. "No, he and Fiona have a thing."

"Is one of those girls Fiona?"

Kaylee shook her head. "She's a cheerleader. The football team made it to the playoffs, so the cheerleaders still have practice after school."

Good to know. The students who'd regularly hung out in the afternoons at the coffee shop in the city hadn't been involved in sports. They'd mostly been glad to be free from the grind of school for an hour or two.

She gestured to the teens. "So this group…they aren't in sports?"

Kaylee kept her voice low. "Tanner's on the rodeo team. That's in the spring. He's really good. Sasha's in drama club. She had the lead role in the fall play. And Bryce and Willow both do track."

Bridget was impressed Kaylee knew so much. "You've lived here for what, three months or so?"

"Yeah."

"Who do you hang out with?"

"I mostly go home after school."

The teens got up, put their mugs in the bin near the trash and left as noisily as they'd arrived. Tanner paused to turn back and say goodbye to Kaylee. She gave him a weak wave, and he exited behind the rest of them.

"Are you sure he's serious with the girl—what was her

name?" Bridget brought a towel and cleaner to the table with Kaylee on her heels.

"Fiona. Yes. They're solid."

"Well, he was pretty friendly with you." She cleaned the table and returned to the counter.

"He's like that with everyone. He's popular, but not a jerk. He's just…nice."

"Nice is the best way to be." Bridget gave her a smile. She couldn't help thinking the description fit Mac, too. Popular. Not a jerk. Just…nice. She really needed to stop thinking about him. "Now, let me show you how to make the cappuccino…"

Over the next hour, more teens and a few employees from nearby businesses stopped in, and she showed Kaylee how to make various drinks and described what her expectations were in regard to cleaning the tables, taking cash and other odds and ends.

"What if someone orders something I don't know how to make?" Kaylee nibbled on her fingernail.

"I'll be here. Don't worry."

"What if there's a long line?"

"We'll handle each customer one by one. It happens."

When the final customer walked out the door, Kaylee sat on one of the stools and seemed to wither. "There's a lot to learn."

"Yep. And you'll be fine. I know it takes time to get comfortable with everything. Don't worry about it, okay?"

Her pinched expression told Bridget she was worried about it.

"You should sell cookies or brownies or something." Kaylee pointed to the empty glass case.

"I know. Sawyer and Tess said the same thing. I'm only good at baking the basics, though, and I don't know anybody I could buy them from."

"Baking's easy. I watched the cooking shows with my mom after school. We baked all kinds of stuff."

Bridget liked the idea of baking things herself, but would anyone buy what she made? It wasn't as though she'd ever worked for a bakery or anything. She'd checked Wyoming's laws before moving here, so she knew it was legal.

"You could at least sell cookies," Kaylee said. "We're always starving when we get out of school."

Bridget rubbed her chin, considering it. "I think you're right. I'll try to make something tonight."

"Either make the cookies super big or make them bite-size. Then you can package like six of the minis together." Kaylee grew more animated. "Back in Dallas, Mom and I always bought the packages of small cookies to split, and the guys always went for the giant ones."

"Good to know." She slung a fresh towel over her shoulder and opened the dishwasher. "Thanks for sharing your opinion with me. I appreciate it."

Kaylee blushed. She turned as the bell clanged again and Mac strode inside, his expression equally hopeful and wary. Bridget's pulse quickened as he neared.

Kaylee checked her phone. "Five already?"

Bridget couldn't believe it, either. The day had flown by.

"How was the grand opening?" Mac stood on the other side of the counter while Kaylee headed to the back to get her things.

"Really good." Bridget began unloading the dishwasher, drying the mugs where water droplets had pooled.

"I'm glad to hear it." He kept his voice low. "How did Kaylee do?"

"She'll get the hang of it."

"What does that mean?" He frowned.

"It means she's smart and eager to learn."

"Oh." His face cleared. Kaylee returned wearing a coat and carrying her backpack.

"Should I wash this at home?" She held up the apron.

"No, leave it with me. I'll wash it." Bridget reached out to take it. "You did good today, Kaylee. I'll see you on Wednesday."

Kaylee smiled shyly and thanked her. She and Mac said goodbye and left as Bridget continued putting away dishes. Once Kaylee and Mac were headed toward the truck, she locked the front door, turned the Open sign to Closed and surveyed the shop.

Today had been a success.

She hoped it wasn't a fluke. If she could attract a group of regular customers, the shop would easily support her.

And Kaylee was on to something with the baked goods. Bridget could bake a few dozen cookies after supper. Everyone liked chocolate chip, right?

Then she remembered she didn't even have the ingredients on hand to bake anything, and there was no way she was hiking the mile to the grocery store tonight.

She untied her apron. She needed a car. And she needed her driver's license.

But before she could get either, she had to learn how to drive.

With a sigh, she scratched the idea of baking for the moment. What she could do, though, was print out some easy recipes and make a list of ingredients to purchase. Any additional revenue stream would help her.

She'd been out on the streets once. She'd never let that happen again.

Kaylee wasn't going to be happy with him.

Friday night at five, Mac pulled into his usual parking spot near Brewed Awakening. Kaylee had volunteered to work after school today since the high school crowd had made the coffee shop their after-school hangout. The football team had lost last week, so all the students would be in town.

He'd been pleasantly surprised that Kaylee had gone to school every day this week and had only had one meltdown about work when he'd picked her up on Wednesday. She'd climbed into the truck and announced she'd never be able to learn how to make all those drinks. Apparently, she'd added two pumps of the wrong type of syrup into one of her classmate's frappés, and it had been mortifying. Her words, not his.

Mac had patiently told her mistakes happen, and she'd actually glared at him. Well, she was going to be glaring at him even harder on the way home when he told her he'd signed her up for driver's training starting next week. She'd been fighting him on this for two months, but it was time for her to get her permit. She'd be sixteen soon, and he wouldn't always be able to drive her everywhere she wanted to go.

Honestly, he didn't have the time to drive her everywhere.

Maybe if he promised her a new car to go with the license…

He got out of the truck and stretched his arms over his head. It had been a long day in the saddle. The weather had dipped into the low thirties. Some Novembers arrived with barely a whimper, and others arrived with bitter temps. This one was going to be cold.

Half expecting to hear someone calling his name to ask him for a donation, he hustled to the coffee shop entrance and opened the door. Thankfully, no one flagged him down. He'd fielded another call from Dina about the football uniforms as well as two other calls from locals this week. He hadn't responded to any of them.

"Hi, Mac!" Kaylee waved.

The final customer passed him as Mac continued to the counter and sat on a stool. "Hey, Kay, how was school?"

"Fine. I'm glad it's Friday, though. Give me a sec, okay?" She held up a finger before disappearing through the doorway to the back room.

"Want a cup before I toss it? On the house." Bridget held up a to-go cup. Her eyes shimmered with something he couldn't put his finger on. Contentment? Eagerness? Whatever it was, it sure looked good on her. Her typical work outfit did, too. He couldn't stop staring at the silver necklace she always wore. It had a charm, but he couldn't figure out what it was. A bird of some sort.

"No, thanks. It'll keep me up all night."

"I already *am* up all night," she said under her breath.

"Why? What's going on?"

"Oh, sorry. You weren't supposed to hear that." She placed the cup on top of the stack nearby. "I don't know how you all do it around here. It's so quiet. Well, except for the wind or the animals howling."

"The wind kept you up last night?"

"Try most nights. But other things keep me up, too."

He looked at her more carefully and noted the slight bags under her eyes. "Like what?"

"The silence. It's creepy."

"Isn't silence supposed to help you sleep?"

"Not when I'm used to city sounds."

"Ah." He couldn't stop his grin. "You know what you need? A white-noise machine."

"I have an app on my phone." She wiped the counter and tossed the cloth into a bin. "It's not working."

"Hmm…" He didn't know what would work then. "Give

it time. The noises will seem normal after a while. The silence, too."

"I'm ready." Kaylee bounced over to him. "Are you sure you won't get pizza with us, Bridget?"

Please say no. Mac held his breath, knowing Kaylee had asked her twice this week.

"Not tonight. I'm trying those recipes we talked about." Her warm smile made his stomach flip. Weird.

"You can bake later." Kaylee gave her a pleading look, but Bridget shook her head. "Well, maybe you could come over and see the ranch tomorrow."

"Sorry, I can't. I'm working."

"Next week?"

Mac cleared his throat. "Actually, Kaylee, Saturdays won't work."

"Why not?"

"Well, for one, Bridget has to work, but two, I signed you up for driver's training."

"You did what?" Her expression of horror didn't shock him. He'd known this wouldn't go over well. He probably should have waited until they were alone, though, to tell her. She shook her head in disgust. "None of the kids around here go to driver's ed. They get their permits, and their parents teach them. Why do I have to take classes?"

"Because I want you to be safe. I'm not budging on this." He'd budged on too many things already. Auto safety wasn't something he was willing to skimp on.

"I'm not going." Her chin jutted high.

"I found a class that meets on Tuesdays, Thursdays and Saturdays. You'll be done on Thanksgiving weekend." He gestured for her to head to the door, but she stood her ground.

Bridget approached, wiping her hands with her apron. "Is there room left in the class?"

Both he and Kaylee stared at her.

"I think so, why?" Mac asked.

She hesitated. "I need to get my license, too, and I have no idea how to get started."

"Really?" Kaylee looked like she'd seen a giraffe walking down Main Street. "You don't know how to drive?"

"Nope."

"Why not?"

"Because I didn't need to drive in the city. I could walk most places, and they had public transportation if I couldn't. Plus, no one I knew had a car."

"Oh." Kaylee moved closer to her. "We'll do it together. Mac will take us. And he'll show us both how to drive, won't you?"

They directed their attention to him, and he shifted his weight from one foot to the other. What had he gotten himself into? It was one thing to enroll his sister in driver's ed and teach her how to drive. It was another thing entirely to add Bridget to the mix.

"That's kind of you, Kaylee," Bridget said as her lashes lowered. "But if I could get a ride to the classes with you, I'm sure Sawyer would teach me the driving part."

Yes, Sawyer would, but for whatever reason, Mac didn't like that idea, either.

"I'll teach you both," he said gruffly. Great. Now he was going to be spending even more time with Bridget.

"You don't have to…"

"I want to. If I'm getting Kaylee behind the wheel, it won't be hard to get you behind it, too. It'll save time, teaching you both at once."

Her expression softened, and the way she was looking at him made him feel like a hero. Her gratitude made him uncomfortable.

He wasn't doing this for her. He was doing this for Kaylee.

"Who do I call to sign up?" She took out her phone, her finger poised over it.

"I'll text you the info," he said. "You'll both need to get your permits on Monday, though."

"I'll never pass the test." Kaylee tipped her head back dramatically. "The booklet is like fifty pages long."

"Don't they have sample tests?" Mac asked. "I'm sure they do. Just read through the booklet and take the practice test. You'll do okay."

"What if I fail?"

He let out a sigh. "Study this weekend. If you fail, you can retake it, okay?"

"Can I go with you to get the permit?" Bridget's nose crinkled.

"Of course." Mac felt bad that she thought she had to ask. It couldn't be easy having to rely on other people to get you where you needed to be.

"Thanks." She met his eyes again, and a zip of warmth spread through his body. As much as he told himself he was including Bridget for Kaylee's sake, he knew deep down there was more to it.

He wanted to be the one to teach her how to drive. He wanted to spend more time with her.

Bridget appealed to him.

He'd better not get carried away. He had too much to think about already. The ranch. His sister. The money. The requests for donations. The calves.

Women are going to walk all over you, boy.

Yeah, well, not if he had anything to say about it. He'd teach Bridget how to drive, and then he'd retreat to his normal, solitary routine. If he still had one.

Chapter Four

The following Tuesday morning Bridget bagged freshly ground coffee beans and listened with half an ear to the conversation and guffaws of the four elderly gentlemen sitting at the table in the far corner. They'd quickly become regulars, showing up every weekday around nine and staying for a few hours. Lyle, John, Alan and Joe. She smiled to herself. Her guys.

A decade of working in diners and coffee shops had tuned her in to loneliness. She was thankful she could provide a place for them to gather together, and in the process, feel less alone herself. Like many around here, they'd been curious about her, and she'd told them the stuff she didn't mind people knowing. They'd been content with that.

The scraping of chairs alerted her the guys were on the move. She checked the time. Eleven. The hours passed quickly when the shop was busy. And it had been busy every day. Which brought another concern front and center—what was she going to do about the next three Saturday mornings? She couldn't run Brewed Awakening *and* attend driver's training classes. Kaylee was the only other person who knew how to run the shop, and she'd be with Bridget.

Last Saturday's sales had been terrific. She couldn't afford to close the place and potentially lose repeat business. Not now, not when she was just starting out.

Yesterday afternoon she'd had to close early so Mac could take her and Kaylee to the DMV to get their permits. Thankfully, they'd both passed. Excitement mounted at the thought of the official paperwork folded in her purse.

But getting behind the wheel and actually driving? Made her nervous. More than nervous. Terrified.

"Enjoy the rest of your day." Bridget waved to three of the men as they slowly made their way to the door. After sealing the bag of ground coffee, she began the exciting task of filling an empty sugar packet holder.

"What's your special drink going to be next week? Something fancy?" Joe Schlock always lingered after the other guys left. If Bridget had to guess, she'd put him a few inches shy of six feet tall. Wiry frame, slight potbelly. He kept his thinning gray hair trimmed short and tended to wear jeans and flannel shirts. She'd talked to him enough to know he'd recently turned eighty, lived alone, missed his deceased wife terribly and loved to chat.

She didn't mind. The kind of loneliness he dealt with was etched deep inside her, too.

"I haven't decided yet." Bridget turned her attention to the board with the menu items. With Thanksgiving only a few weeks away, maybe a twist on something pumpkin spice would be in order.

"Linda lived for her coffee." Joe pulled out a stool and sat.

Bridget sighed in contentment as she prepared herself for a long-winded trip down memory lane about his late wife. She absolutely loved hearing him talk about Linda. Personally, she hoped if love ever did find her, she'd find someone who adored her the way Joe had adored Linda.

"The second time her cancer came back, I ordered one of those fancy espresso machines, not as top-of-the-line as yours, mind you." Joe looked at the machine behind her. "Every morning I'd ask her what kind she wanted, and she'd tell me to surprise her."

"Did you?" Bridget asked. He hadn't told her about the espresso machine before. It was kind of difficult to picture him making coffee drinks. He seemed more outdoorsy. "Surprise her, I mean?"

"Of course." He propped his elbow on the counter and waved dismissively. "Had to get creative. I ordered a book with all kinds of recipes, and I ordered all the flavored syrups I thought she'd like. It took some doing because I wasn't used to buying stuff from the computer. Had to ask a pal to help me figure it out."

The thought of Joe going to such lengths to make his wife a little happier during cancer treatments brought a lump to Bridget's throat. That was love.

"What were her favorites?"

"She loved peppermint. And chocolate." His crooked, bony index finger pointed her way. "And she was partial to a coconut mocha almond latte I made up by accident one time. It tasted like one of those candy bars."

"Mmm…that sounds delicious. I might need to get your recipe."

He tapped his finger to his temple. "It's all up here. First you take the coconut-flavored syrup…" He proceeded to explain the ingredients and how he made the drink, step-by-step, and she could see he knew his stuff.

As Joe moved on to describe another drink—what he called a cappucinn-Joe—she tuned out to pray silently. *Lord, You knew I needed someone to watch the store on Saturdays, and here's Joe, who just happens to know how to make coffee drinks. An answer to a prayer I didn't even make. Thank You.*

"...the secret's in the heavy cream. I ran out of milk..." Joe went off on a tangent about a dairy farm his friend in Indiana owned, and when he was finished, Bridget clasped her hands below her chin and captured his gaze.

"Are you busy on Saturday mornings until the end of the month?" she asked.

He frowned, thinking a second, and shook his head. "No, I can't say I am."

"I'm in a bind. I have—" she hesitated, not wanting to give out any more personal information than necessary "—an appointment, but I don't have anyone to run the coffee shop for me."

"I heard you got your driver's permit. You signed up for classes, too, didn't you?"

Taken aback, she had no idea how to respond. How had he found that out?

"Jane Tooly said she saw you and Mac's little sister there yesterday. Jane's mom's plates expired, and they had to get those taken care of because the new cop pulled her over and it put her mother in a tizzy—Jane's words, not mine. He sure has ruffled a lot of feathers, and..."

Was there anything that didn't get noticed and passed on around here?

"...Miss Davies told Lyle's sister—she is one of the nicest ladies you'll ever meet. Crochets little dishcloths and sells them at the bazaar every year—anyway, she said the driver's ed class had almost filled up and a certain newcomer in town was on the list."

"Oh, I see." She hadn't realized how connected everyone in town was and how quickly news spread. Like a grease fire. An out-of-control one at that.

"You don't have anyone to watch the shop, huh? I can

see where that would be a problem." He rubbed his chin, staring thoughtfully at the counter. "I don't suppose Riley Sampson would help you out. She's not too happy you opened the place, but I can't think of anyone else who would know how to brew those drinks on your menu."

The last person she'd ever ask to watch the store was Riley Sampson. The woman had come into the shop last week with a chip on her shoulder and a rude comment for everything. She'd turned her nose up at the menu, then complained loudly to her two companions—both in their late twenties like her—about the prices. She'd even pretended to swipe dirt off the counter with her index finger before the three of them left without ordering a thing.

"I don't think you understand," Bridget said, trying to get the conversation back on track. "I'm talking about *you*, Joe. Would you be interested in running the place for me? You'd have to open it, but I'd be back around noon. I'm not going to sugarcoat it, though—the place will be busy and you'll be the only employee. I know it's a lot to ask."

He blinked rapidly, frowned as if confused and then a grin spread slowly across his face. "You want me to run it?" He jabbed his thumb into his chest. "Me?"

"Yes." She nodded.

"You're sure? I mean, I made Linda her coffee drinks, but I've never made them for anyone else, and she liked them, but she didn't have any other options and she might have just been saying she liked them and I—"

"Yes, I'm sure. I could use the help."

"You realize I'm eighty." He was either trying to talk her out of asking him or trying to convince himself she was serious. She guessed it was the latter.

"Yeah," Bridget said. "I know."

"Imagine that." He straightened, his face clearing. "You know most people get tired of me hanging around them.

I know I talk too much, but I can't seem to help it. I don't remember a time someone wanted me around more, instead of trying to get away from me."

She let out a light laugh, although it did scrape her heart a bit.

"Well, I need you around more. If all goes well, I'll finish the driver's education classes the Saturday of Thanksgiving weekend."

"Your daddy didn't teach you to drive?"

Her daddy hadn't taught her much of anything. Hadn't protected her, either. She wished he would have done a lot of things differently when he'd been alive, like opened his eyes to how her stepmother treated her.

"No, he didn't."

"Well, I'm sure they do it different up in the city." He looked sheepish.

She wouldn't argue with that. "He died when I was twelve."

"I'm mighty sorry to hear that."

A slip on her part. Her parents weren't a topic she discussed with anyone. Her childhood wasn't either. "Do you have any time this week for me to train you on the register?"

"Do I have any time this week? Pshaw…all I've got is time. Let me grab a bite to eat and I'll be back in a jiffy."

"Oh. Okay." She hadn't expected him to come back today, but she supposed the sooner she showed him how everything worked, the better. "Don't rush. We have plenty of time."

"If you start training me and change your mind, I'll understand." He stood, giving her an earnest stare.

"I'm not going to change my mind." Her heart pinched. She knew how he was feeling. She knew it well. For two years after getting her first job, she'd worried every single day about getting fired. All due to insecurity.

"I won't let you down, Bridget."

"See you after lunch." She waved to him as he turned to leave.

One problem solved.

A cluster of other problems remained, though. The progress of making her apartment cozy was on hold. She'd ordered lamps and a rug from an online store, but they wouldn't be in until next week. She still wasn't sleeping well, and there wasn't much she could do about it. And Operation Baked Goods was an ongoing experiment at this point. She'd baked muffins and cookies, but her displays and packaging were nothing special.

People had been buying them, though, so at least there was that. Maybe when the cellophane packaging, black ribbon and oval labels she'd ordered arrived, the treats would look more appealing.

The bell clanged and a group of ladies she didn't recognize chatted all the way to the counter. One of them wrinkled her nose at the lopsided applesauce muffins. Two of the women kept talking while the others eyed the menu.

"I am so glad Joe didn't see us. We would have never gotten away from him." The older woman with poofy white hair and bright red lipstick shook her head. "I ran into him at the supermarket last week. I kept pushing my cart, or I would have never gotten my shopping done. He followed me down two aisles. I was quite curt with him. Joe has no ability to pick up on other people's signals..."

The woman behind her—slightly younger and more stylish—pushed to the front and proceeded to order a complicated coffee drink, so Bridget missed the rest of their conversation.

As she began making the drink, doubts crept in about

hiring Joe. He'd admitted he couldn't help himself from talking too much. While Bridget didn't mind, other people around here obviously did.

He knew how to make the coffee drinks, though. That was what was important. Right? Would people avoid Brewed Awakening on Saturday mornings if they knew he was in charge?

Gritting her teeth, she returned to the task at hand. She didn't have any alternatives at this point. And she'd already assured him she wouldn't change her mind.

Bridget cashed out the women and bit the inside of her cheek as they laughed and talked on their way to the table near the front.

She had to keep the shop open on Saturday mornings. If Joe drove away her customers, so be it. The last thing she was going to do was break the man's heart.

First up, a hot shower. Wait, he'd forgotten to jot down the blue tag 41 on the whiteboard in the ranch office. Mac ground the heel of his hand into his temple as he stopped in his tracks walking to the house late Tuesday afternoon. He'd add it tomorrow morning. Every bone in his body ached at the moment.

He'd better set a reminder on his phone. Every calf he'd decided to keep over the winter was too important to let slip through the cracks. Mac took his phone out of his coat pocket and typed in a reminder to check the calf.

His breath spiraled in the air. It had been another long day in the saddle. This time of year always put him on alert. Had he baled enough extra hay over the summer or would he need to supplement with purchased hay? The pastures didn't offer enough forage for his herd to graze all winter.

He didn't want Dad to end up being right that it was foolish to keep those extra calves.

Mac marched on toward the house, eyeing the sky. What was the weather forecast? The threat of early winter storms put him on edge. Didn't seem to be one brewing, though.

Kaylee had gotten a ride home from school earlier, so at least he hadn't had to drop everything to drive into town for once, but even with the extra hour on the ranch, he couldn't shake the feeling he was behind.

As he reached for the side door leading to the house, the rumble of a vehicle in the driveway got his attention. A black truck stopped. Out stepped John Lutz. The man ambled toward him.

Mac really didn't have the energy for this. He barely had time to get cleaned up before he had to pick up Bridget and drop her and Kaylee off at the community center where their driver's ed classes were being held.

"What can I do for you, John?" He tried to keep his tone pleasant, but his insides begged for this encounter to be over with ASAP.

"I've got those quotes I mentioned. The estimated expenses to repair the irrigation diversion." John held out a stack of papers, pointing to a column on the left of the top page. "It's pretty self-explanatory, but we can go inside and I'll walk you through it if you'd like."

"Not necessary," Mac said a little too quickly. "I'm sure I'll have no problem figuring it out."

"If you have any questions, I can help." John frowned. "Although page three gets a bit tricky. Maybe I should get you up to speed…"

"Actually, I have to run Kaylee into town soon."

His face brightened. "How is she? I hear she's helping out at the new coffee shop. Mary and I need to get over there soon."

"She's good." At the very least, improving. "She's taking driver's ed classes, so…"

"You're not gonna teach her yourself?" He scratched his stubble.

"I think it's best left to the professionals." He aimed for good-natured in his reply, but he inwardly bristled. Sure, most of the locals skipped formal training and taught their kids how to drive, but he was new to this. He didn't want to take the chance he'd teach her wrong or forget something important and be the reason she got in an accident.

Kaylee was the only family he had left, and he wanted her around until they were both old.

"You might have a point, there." John chuckled. "Those Danbury kids sure could have used lessons. I don't know if their ma and pa taught them a lick about driving. I've seen the youngest hot-rodding out on Old Bend Road more than once."

Terrific. Now he had to worry about other drivers on the road, too. Until this point, he'd only been worried about Kaylee. Mac glanced down at the papers he was holding and moved them to his other hand.

He didn't have time for chitchat. The moment grew awkward, then John pointed to the estimates. "Holler if you have any questions."

"I will." He exhaled in relief when John turned and strolled back to the truck.

Mac didn't even wait until John started up the truck before heading into the house. He hung up his coat in the mudroom and massaged his neck while heading down the hallway.

"Come on! We're going to be late." Kaylee sat on the couch and shoved one foot into a running shoe.

He tossed the stack of papers onto the console table and kept walking.

"Mac!"

Stopping, he fought a groan and let his head drop back.

He was taking five minutes to clean up in the shower and if it made them late, they'd be late. There was no way he was getting in the truck smelling like a pile of manure.

"I'll be ready in five minutes." He was surprised he sounded so calm. "Grab a bite to eat while you're waiting, okay?"

"I thought we were stopping to get tacos."

"No time." His stomach grumbled at the thought of tacos. "We'll get something to eat after your class."

"Promise?"

"Promise."

She'd be starving by then, no doubt, but what else could he do? He'd lost track of time, and then John had stopped by and…

From the minute he'd arrived here to live full-time as a freshman in high school, Mac had immersed himself in the ranch. He doubted he would change. Didn't want to, either.

Until recently, it had been fine for him to spend all day checking cattle and doing chores. He'd never had anyone else depending on him. But with Kaylee here…

The ranch didn't run itself.

So why did he feel guilty doing his job?

Because you have the money to hire more people if you really want to, but you don't want to, do you?

Shutting his bedroom door, he faced the truth. The ranch was his first love. It mattered to him in a way his father had never understood. Mac might have more on his plate now that Kaylee was living here, but it didn't make the ranch any less important to him.

The cattle, the land, the equipment and everything on this patch of Wyoming depended on him. He hadn't let them down yet, and he had no intention of letting them down ever. He'd just have to take each new challenge one step at a time.

* * *

Bridget's eyes were glazed over as she and Kaylee stepped into Mac's truck after the first driver's ed class ended. Talk about information overload. This whole getting-her-driver's-license thing was turning out to be a big headache.

"Thanks a lot, Mac." Kaylee sounded disgusted. "You officially found us the most boring instructor on the planet." The girl climbed into the back seat, leaving Bridget to buckle into the passenger seat.

"I'm sorry?" He waited for them to get settled before backing out of the parking spot.

Bridget rested the side of her head against the glass and stared up at the stars. They were so bright. There had to be a bajillion up there. She'd never dreamed the sky could display such a magnificent show. Back home, the city lights had dimmed the stars.

"I'm starving," Kaylee announced. "We're getting tacos, Bridget."

"Yum." She didn't have the energy to protest, and besides, she really loved tacos.

"I can drop you off first, if you want." Mac looked her way. Bridget let out the teensiest of sighs. Even in her tired state, her body hummed at seeing his perfect face and hearing his low, smooth voice. She gulped. Maybe she should get dropped off.

But tacos…so yummy…

"If you're hungry, you're welcome to join us." He turned onto a side street.

"I'm hungry." She didn't even try to deny it. She was hungry for more than tacos—she craved companionship. She didn't want to be alone right now. Which was odd, since she'd literally been around people since opening the shop at seven this morning. Normally, being alone didn't bother her.

"I'm famished," Kaylee said dramatically.

"We know, all right?" Mac flashed her a grin in the rearview.

Bridget liked the way they teased each other.

"Let's hope Rex still has tacos left from the Tuesday rush…" He turned into the parking lot behind the Barking Squirrel, and the three of them got out of the truck. Bridget rubbed her forearms. Even wearing her winter coat, she felt chilled.

Mac held the restaurant door open for them, and they found a booth along the wall. The place was emptying out—clearly the dinner rush had come and gone. A waitress stopped by wearing a red polo shirt and jeans. They all ordered tacos and sodas, and Mac requested queso and chips as an appetizer.

"I don't think I can sit through thirty hours of these classes." As soon as the waitress arrived with their drinks, Kaylee tore the paper off her straw.

"You'd be surprised at what you can sit through." Mac sat across from Bridget and Kaylee, and Bridget couldn't help but stare at him. He was even more attractive in close quarters.

Who was she kidding? He was a fine-looking man in any quarters.

"I can barely sit through biology every day," Kaylee said. "Now this? Uh-uh. Braxton was right. Driver's ed is a waste of time."

"Braxton Crossdale?" Mac snorted. "I wouldn't listen to that kid."

"Well, I don't have much of a choice. He's my lab partner."

"I've seen him drive, Kay." He leaned over the table. "The kid hits every curb he comes across. His front end will have to be replaced by the new year if he keeps it up."

Bridget sipped her drink, thankful Mac and Kaylee were comfortable enough with each other to push each other's buttons. She, personally, had never felt safe pushing anyone's buttons, not after spending years trying to avoid her stepmother's rages.

All the times she'd been screamed at, locked in her room for no reason, forced to scrub bathroom floors with a toothbrush… Bridget shook away the horrible memories. She was certain the woman had had an undiagnosed mental disorder, but little good the information did her now.

Hopefully, the queso would come soon. As if the waitress heard her, a platter of nacho chips and cheesy dip appeared in the center of the table. Three hands dove in immediately.

"Delaney said only rich kids go to driver's ed." Kaylee crunched on a chip.

"Tell her only smart kids go." Cheese dripped off the end of the chip he was holding and fell with a plop onto the table.

"Her mom and dad made her drive the country roads by their house."

"Well, you'll be doing the same soon," he said. "When we have a little free time, I'll teach you the basics."

Bridget was on her fifth chip. Or sixth? Who cared. She took another bite.

The thought of actually driving a car brought goose bumps to her arms. When would she learn the basics? Was it even possible for her to learn them? The idea of operating a vehicle intimidated her beyond belief.

"It won't matter," Kaylee mumbled.

"Why?" Mac straightened in his seat.

Kaylee shrugged. "Never mind."

"Something's going on. Tell me." He sipped his drink.

"It's just…everyone looks at me weird."

"What do you mean?"

Kaylee's face flushed as she munched on a chip, clearly avoiding answering the question.

"Because you're taking driver's ed classes?" Mac's eyebrows drew together.

"Not just that. It's…everything."

Bridget figured it was time to join the conversation. "I get weird looks, too, Kaylee. Don't sweat it. Sunrise Bend doesn't get a lot of new people. They'll get used to us."

"You think so?" She brightened and reached for another chip.

"Yeah." Bridget nudged her elbow into Kaylee's arm. "Oh, look, the tacos are here."

Plates filled with hard-shelled tacos, beans and rice were placed before them, and they all attacked their food.

"If anyone makes you uncomfortable, let me know." Mac gave Kaylee a stern look between bites. "I'll take care of it. The Crossdale kid better lay off."

She blanched. "No. No. I don't want you to say anything to anyone. Promise me, Mac."

Oh boy. Bridget kept chewing, willing Mac to say the right thing.

"If you're being harassed…" he said.

"I'm not."

"If that changes…"

"I'll tell you." Kaylee nodded.

"Okay." Mac's jaw tightened. "You know, I've been in your shoes before."

"I doubt it," Kaylee said under her breath.

Bridget watched the exchange with unabashed fascination as she shoveled another forkful of rice into her mouth.

"I moved to Sunrise Bend when I was fourteen." He gave Kaylee the look that said you need to listen. He glanced at Bridget, too, but she wasn't sure what his expression was telling her. "I'd spent the previous two summers on the ranch with Otis and Helen—I don't think you met her before she died. Anyhow, I did not want to go to the college prep high school Dad had picked out for me. I'd gotten to know Austin, Jet and Sawyer when I was here the previous summer, and I wanted to go to high school with them and work on the ranch with Otis. So I told Dad."

"I didn't know that's how you ended up here." Kaylee picked up her second taco. "I can't believe Dad actually let you move. You were younger than me."

"It was not a good conversation." His eyes grew hooded as if the memories were painful. Bridget took another bite. Interesting. His life wasn't as perfect as she'd previously assumed. "The first day of high school, the kids in the hallway parted like a zipper when I walked in. They all stared at me and whispered. I never felt so out of place in my life."

"That's what they did to me, too," Kaylee said softly.

"I'm sorry. For both of you," Bridget said, meaning it.

Kaylee flashed a grateful smile to her. Mac did, too.

"For a long time," Mac said, "all I heard were cracks about how nice it must be to have a rich father. But after a while, they got to know me. And they realized the only thing different about me was the fact my dad had a lot of money. They got used to me, and they'll get used to you, too."

Bridget took another drink. She didn't want to feel sorry for Mac, but she kind of did. Of course, it was nothing like what she'd been through. But still.

"What if they don't?" Kaylee asked.

"You'll always have me."

With her eyes burning, Bridget turned her attention to her plate. That's what made her different from Mac. Different from Kaylee.

They had each other.

And she'd been tossed out on her own. Alone. Like garbage.

Sixteen years old. She'd been sixteen when her stepmother threw her out with no money, no warning. That late May afternoon had been one of the worst of her life.

Mac and Kaylee would never know how it felt to have nothing and no one. To be on the streets. And she was glad. She didn't want anyone to ever go through what she had been through. They'd had cushions to break their fall—money and loved ones.

When a person had no cushions…well, the fall might not kill you, but it left parts of you broken, never to be put back together.

She pushed her plate away. She wasn't hungry anymore. A lot had changed in ten years. She had more options than when she was sixteen.

But she'd keep her past tucked in her pocket where it belonged.

Chapter Five

"Okay, who wants to go first?" Mac asked.

He held the driver's-side door open in the church parking lot on Thursday after Bridget closed Brewed Awakening. She and Kaylee were huddled together staring at his truck like it was a snarling wolf. Kaylee's mitten-clad fists propped up her chin as she shook her head, while Bridget looked as if she'd prefer cutting off her own finger to having her first driving lesson.

Truth be told, he didn't want to teach either of them how to drive any more than they wanted to get in the truck. What if he forgot something major and they crashed it?

He wasn't a driving instructor. He was just a cowboy in way over his head.

"Well, one of you is going to have to get in at some point." He gestured to the open door. "Who's first?"

"You go, Bridget." Kaylee pushed her forward. "I'm too nervous."

"I wouldn't want to take your spot." Bridget hung back. "You're the top priority here."

Mac groaned and stared at the sky. Why him? Maybe he should have asked Otis to teach these two the way the old-timer had taught him. Not that Mac personally remembered much of the training. It seemed like he'd been driving his entire life.

"You wouldn't be taking my spot," Kaylee said. "I learn better watching someone else. Plus, my stomach feels funny. I don't want to throw up."

"Don't even think about throwing up in my truck." Mac tried not to glare, but he did not do vomit.

"I feel gaggy."

"Do we need to go home?" After a full week of her going to school every day, he didn't want to retrigger the cycle of her not feeling good and staying home. But if she thought she was going to hurl…

"No."

"Well, I don't want anyone puking. Kay, get in the back." Mac turned to Bridget. "Looks like you're up."

She stared blankly and appeared ready to argue with him. But then she climbed into the seat while he jogged around to the passenger side. Once he got settled, Mac looked back at Kaylee, who did look nauseous.

"I mean it, Kay, don't yack in here." He hated to even say it, but he could not handle vomit in his truck. He'd never get the smell out.

"She's not sick, Mac. It's nerves." Bridget's tongue had finally loosened. Her hands were folded on her lap. The seat was a good fifteen miles from the steering wheel.

"Reach down with your left hand," he said. "You'll feel a lever along the side of the seat. If you push it forward, the seat will move toward the steering wheel. Push it backward and it will reverse."

Bridget fumbled to find it, getting startled when the seat slowly began moving with an electronic droning noise. "How far should it go?"

"Until your foot is comfortable on the gas pedal."

"Which one's the gas pedal?" The seat kept moving.

He scooted over, although the console between them limited how far he could go. "The pedal farthest to the right. The one next to it—the one in the middle there—that's the brake. You press on the gas to go, and you press on the brake to stop."

"Gas pedal, go. Brake, stop. Got it."

Her body was crammed against the wheel and her knees were practically touching the front panel. He wasn't sure if he wanted to laugh at how absurd she looked or pinch the bridge of his nose in frustration. "Ease back a little. You're way too close."

"What do you mean?" Her brown eyes swirled with worry.

"The wheel. The pedals. You want to be comfortable, not packed in like a sardine."

The electronic noise commenced again, and she backed up the seat fraction by fraction. It took two years. He checked his watch. At this point, neither Kaylee nor Bridget would actually start the truck until their driver's ed classes were over.

"Comfortable?" he asked.

"No. I'm not comfortable. My couch is comfortable. This is a giant machine that I'm somehow supposed to operate without crashing and killing us all. You expect me to drive this monster? Hello? I can barely ride a bike."

He hadn't realized it was so intimidating. Maybe slow was the way to go, after all.

"Let's review the basics before you actually operate this—" he lifted his fingers in air quotes "—giant machine, okay?"

Bridget nodded, her lips drawn into a tight line.

"Put your hands on the wheel. Like this."

She shot him a glare but obeyed.

"This is a push start so all you have to do is put your

foot on the brake and press the button there, and the truck will start. Don't do it yet, though."

"Don't worry. I have no desire to bring this beast to life."

He'd ignore that comment.

"First, you want to check your mirrors. Go ahead and adjust the rearview until you can see out the back. The side mirrors are controlled by buttons in the door. See them?" Mac went on to explain the dashboard displays, the windshield wipers, emergency brake and gears. "Okay, I think you're ready. Go ahead and start it up."

Her throat worked as she looked down at her foot, poised on the brake, then she hissed as she pressed the start button. The truck came to life with a low rumble. Her loud sigh of relief made him wonder if she'd expected a bomb to go off rather than the truck to start.

"Good job." He pointed to the shifter. "Go ahead and put it in Drive. You can take us on a tour of the parking lot for a few minutes."

"Drive? Already? Are you kidding me?"

"I'm not kidding."

Her face said it all—this was lunacy.

"Just press the accelerator slowly." The truck leaped forward. He gripped the handle above the door. "Press it gently."

"What do you mean?" Her voice rose in panic. "I'm going way too fast."

He checked the speedometer. She was going seven miles per hour.

"So, slow down."

"How do I slow down?"

"Just ease your foot off the gas. Press the brakes."

She started pressing on the gas pedal with her right foot while simultaneously pressing the brake with her left foot. The truck bucked and made a grinding noise.

"No! Take your foot off the gas pedal. You can't press both at the same time." His heartbeat thumped so hard he could hear it in both ears. "You always, always use your right foot to accelerate *and* to brake. You never use both feet, and you never press both at once."

As the truck stopped, Bridget's face drained of color, and her knuckles were white on the wheel.

He covered her right hand with his own. "It's okay. No harm done. Try it again."

"No harm done?" she yelled. "I almost killed us, and you want me to try it again? Are you out of your mind?"

"You didn't almost kill anyone. It was an honest mistake." Mac was trying to be patient, but he clearly was not cut out for this. "Just try again. It will be fine."

She glared at him but pressed on the gas pedal. The truck lurched forward a few feet, then a few more as she got used to it.

"Turn the wheel to the right—slowly—and we'll go in a circle." Mac's hand was near the steering wheel in case he needed to take charge, but Bridget had no trouble steering it. She drove around the empty lot once before he told her to press the brake to come to a stop. It was a jerky stop, but the truck halted. "Want to go again?"

She shook her head, her lips bluish, so he figured it was Kaylee's turn. "Put the truck in park, and let's get Kaylee up here." He looked back to where his sister clutched her seat belt and stared at him through round, terrified eyes.

Bridget climbed out of the truck. Her cheeks expanded as she puffed out a breath and bent over to brace her hands on her thighs.

"Come on. It's your turn." He patted the driver's seat. Kaylee grimaced, shaking her head.

"You can do the same as Bridget," he said. "It's easy."

"No, thank you." Then she pressed her stomach and groaned. Was she going to throw up?

"Never mind," he said. "You'll drive next time."

Bridget opened the back door, popping her head into the truck to speak to Kaylee. "I know you're nervous, but maybe you should get it over with. It's not going to get easier if you wait."

"If she doesn't want to do it, she doesn't have to." Mac didn't like when Bridget pressured Kaylee. Couldn't she see his sister might hurl?

"The instructor is making us drive next week." Bridget's color had returned, and Mac had to admit the rosiness in her cheeks made her prettier than ever. She addressed Kaylee again. "Wouldn't you rather have your first time here? With us?"

He opened his mouth to defend his sister, but Kaylee actually stepped out of the back seat. Then she hauled herself into the driver's seat, and Bridget took her spot in the back.

"You don't have to do this, you know," he said gently. He didn't want to push her too hard.

The vein in her forehead throbbed, and her face was pale, but she placed her hands on the wheel. "Check the mirrors, right?"

Wow, she'd actually listened to him teach Bridget. "Yeah, but I'm serious, Kay. You're upset. We can do this another time."

With her mouth shut, she shook her head. "How do I adjust the seat again?"

He told her, and after having her try out the windshield wipers and locate the gears, he gave her the go ahead to drive. She was marginally better than Bridget, but only by a hair. After she looped around the parking lot, she parked the truck, turned it off, and climbed out. Bridget got out, too.

Mac came around the front to get back into the driver's seat and stopped in his tracks. The girls were hugging and laughing and jumping up and down.

Laughing? Jumping? He found nothing funny about the previous thirty minutes of his life. And then to his amazement, Kaylee yanked on his arm, pulling him over, and yelled, "Group hug."

The three of them embraced. It was over before it began. Then Kaylee was talking a mile a minute, her face bright as the sun, and Bridget was doing the same.

"I thought I was going to drive us right into the side of the church..." Bridget placed her hand over her heart.

"I was afraid I'd flip the truck over when I pressed the brake..." Kaylee sat in the back seat, buckling up.

Driving into the side of the church? Flipping the truck?

Mac shook his head. He was in an alternate universe. It was the only logical explanation for what he'd just witnessed. He drove to the community center. They chattered all the way there.

When he parked, Bridget put her hand on his arm. "Thanks, Mac. I'm sorry about pressing the gas and the brake at the same time. I hope I didn't hurt the truck."

"You didn't hurt anything."

Kaylee opened Bridget's door. "Come on, let's get in there."

Bridget smiled shyly at him, then joined his sister.

As he watched them hurry arm in arm into the building, he realized the adrenaline in his veins was still roaring. From the driving lessons? The group hug? Or from Bridget's smile?

He didn't know, and he didn't want to find out.

"When are you going to decorate this place for Christmas?" Joe asked Friday afternoon.

Bridget made a note in the small binder of drink recipes she'd printed out before turning back to Joe. He'd been stopping in every day after lunch for training, and she'd been impressed at his knowledge of making the various coffee drinks. His understanding of her electronic checkout system, though? He was struggling. Technology and Joe didn't quite mix.

"Christmas?" She tapped her finger to her chin. "I haven't thought about decorating yet. I need to get on it."

"The holiday parade and open house are coming up. You want this place to be festive for it. All the local businesses stay open. Most have cookies and treats." Joe wore his typical flannel shirt and jeans, but he'd tied a denim apron—the same as hers—around his waist. She had to admit he looked right at home working here.

"Holiday open house? I hadn't heard." She supposed she should join the chamber of commerce, but it felt too revealing. Plus, it would likely involve meetings, and she didn't do those. Meetings meant small talk, which led to people asking personal questions or suggesting she volunteer for things she had no desire to be involved with.

The people of Sunrise Bend were still curious about her. But as the days wore on, they seemed to accept her vague answers about her past. And when she asked them about themselves, they quickly moved on to sharing their own stories.

That was the way she liked it. She preferred listening to talking. Being in the shadows rather than the spotlight.

She'd learned a lot about the town in the short time the coffee shop had been open. People here were hard-working and loyal and helped each other out. The previous owners, Marge and Bud Sampson, were well-liked, and the locals mentioned them often. A few people had commented negatively on the way their daughter, Riley, ran the place when she took it over. Bridget just listened politely, but inwardly, she was thankful she hadn't seen Riley again.

"Where are your decorations stored? I can help you put 'em up." Joe dropped wooden coffee stirrers into a metal container. The bell above the door alerted them to a group of teenagers coming in, bringing their fun brand of chaos with them.

"Why don't you take the orders and handle the cash register, while I make the drinks this time?" Bridget said. "Then you'll have the hang of it for tomorrow."

"Yes, ma'am." He saluted her. She arched her eyebrows and suppressed a chuckle. Joe then shuffled to the register where five boys jostled each other. "What can I get you there? Hey, you're Josh and Jenny's boy, aren't you?"

The kid first in line straightened. "Yes, sir."

"Dalton?"

"No, Dalton's my older brother. I'm Bryce."

The boys behind Bryce were joking with each other. The teens had proven to be a key component to her profits. Kaylee's suggestion to bake giant cookies had been genius. Bridget sold at least a dozen to the high school students every day.

"Bryce. That's right." Joe nodded enthusiastically. "You pulled down a ten-point buck on opening weekend. Hawk's Creek, if I'm not mistaken. I've hunted there a time or two in my day…"

"You heard about that?" Bryce's chest puffed out.

"Son, everyone heard about that."

"Yeah, me and my dad went out at four in the morning—"

"Hey, Bryce, order already, will you?" One of the teens pushed to the front to stand next to him. Joe, oblivious to the kid's impatience, continued to talk about all the fawns he'd seen out there this summer.

Bridget debated stepping in to help him take the orders. She didn't want Joe's rambling to drive away these teens. She took pride in her quick service.

"Well, I'd better take your order, or I'll talk all day," Joe said. "Promise to tell me about it later, though, okay? Now, what can I get you?"

Bridget turned to grab a mug, grateful she hadn't had to intervene. She and Joe spent the next ten minutes working together to take care of the group. Joe asked questions whenever he couldn't figure out what button to push. Surprisingly, one of the boys in line explained the credit card reader in a way he understood.

Another group of high schoolers came in as the boys took their coffees to the table near the front window. Joe took their orders and chatted with them, and Bridget realized he seemed to know something about each one, whether it was their parents or something they were involved with in the community.

Joe paid attention to people. He cared.

After the teens were served, Bridget went over the trickier aspects of the checkout screen with him. "Just remember to go to this screen for debit…"

Two older women, deep in conversation, approached. When they reached the counter, Joe greeted them. The moment they realized he would be waiting on them, they exchanged panicked glances.

"Howdy, Brenda. What can I get you?" Joe asked. "Our special is the vanilla chai latte today."

"Oh, ah, yes, that sounds good." The woman looked flustered. She glanced at her companion sharply. "We'll take two." She pointed to the platter where the giant chocolate chip cookies in cellophane bags were arranged. The bite-size sugar cookies were stacked in clear bags, too. "Do you want to split those sugar cookies, Nancy?"

"Sure." The woman gave Joe a worried glance, which Bridget didn't think he noticed. At least, she hoped he hadn't.

"I heard Sam got a flat last week." He frowned as he pressed the screen buttons, having to go back twice. "It was fortunate he didn't slide into the ditch. That stretch of road out on—"

"Yes, Sam had a flat tire," Nancy snapped, arching her eyebrow to her friend as if to say *here we go.*

"It's a shame. I hope it wasn't the big pothole by the Sutton place. The road needs fixing. I keep calling the county—"

"I guess we'll never know." Nancy's tone was positively rude.

Bridget quickly made their drinks and set them on the counter with a tight smile. The women weren't treating Joe well, and it made her feel protective of him.

"Oh, this machine…" He shook his head. "I think I got it now. Credit card? Slide it right in this here slot."

The woman shot him a glare. "I know where it goes, Joe."

Bridget bristled at her rudeness. She'd had her share of off-putting customers over the years, but so far, the locals of Sunrise Bend had been friendly and good-natured. With her. And with Kaylee.

But with Joe?

"I'm sure you do, Nancy." He gave her a good-natured nod. "I'm in training, so you'll have to bear with me."

"Training?" Her expression fairly screamed she'd never come back.

"I'll be running the place on Saturday mornings for a few weeks." He looked over at Bridget warmly. "I'm mighty obliged Bridget here is taking a chance on an old-timer like me."

The woman gave Bridget a cold once-over, slipped her credit card back into her wallet and snatched the to-go cup. "I'll keep that in mind."

She might as well have said *I'll never come in on a Saturday if I have to put up with you.*

"Have a nice day, now." He waved to them as they hurried, straight-backed, to the door.

"Who was that?" Bridget stood next to him, staring as the door closed behind them.

"Nancy Felix and Brenda Daly. They organize a lot of fundraisers and events for the town."

"They seemed kind of…uptight." She didn't want to speak ill of anyone. However, it was the truth.

"Yeah, you don't want them on your bad side. At least, that's what I've been told. Never had a problem with them myself."

Never had a problem with them? Bridget wanted to ask him what about right now?

She didn't, though. She wanted to hug this man with his big, kind heart. He saw the best in people, even when they were rude to his face. She, on the other hand, was not as trusting as he was. Nor was she inclined to see the best in people. Not after what her stepmother had put her through.

If Nancy and Brenda had influence in town and clearly disliked Joe, what would that mean for Brewed Awakening on Saturdays?

There wasn't much she could do if they decided to avoid the coffee shop whenever Joe was working. Besides, in a few short weeks, she wouldn't need the extra help.

The next hour crawled by with few customers. Before Joe left for the night, she gave him her parting instructions on how to open the store in the morning. She was just getting ready to lock the door when Sawyer entered wearing a cowboy hat, boots, jeans and an unzipped jacket. Seeing his lanky frame always brought a smile to her face.

She ran over and gave him a big hug. "What are you doing here? I thought you were busy at the ranch."

"I'm under strict orders to drive you to Mac's. We're all having pizza, and you're not getting out of it this time."

"Oh, no. I'd better not. I have a lot to do around here." She stepped backward. Pizza with all of Sawyer's friends? She wasn't really a socializer. She'd gotten used to staying home by herself or doing things alone.

But since arriving in Sunrise Bend, she hadn't been as content with being alone as she'd been in the city. In some ways the solitude was necessary, but in other ways it was simply easier than putting herself out there.

She couldn't put her whole self out there. She just couldn't.

What if she let her guard down and something embarrassing slipped out? Rejection would be devastating here. This was a small town, one she wanted to live in permanently. There was no room for error on her part.

Sawyer stood there with his head at an angle. He sighed. "Whatever you have to do can wait."

"But then you'd have to drive me back here when you're done."

"Randy and Hannah will take you. She lives up the road at the apartment complex, and Randy's only five minutes further out."

"But—"

"It's Friday." Sawyer's gentle tone dulled her sharp edges. "I want you there. It will give us a chance to catch up along the way. I've missed you, Bridge."

She missed him, too. He'd been her honorary big brother and best friend for a decade. And pizza sounded good. She had to admit she was curious to see where Mac lived.

One of the main reasons she'd moved here was so she could be part of a community. Yeah, a fringe part on the outskirts of the community.

No one here would understand her childhood. Even she didn't understand it.

If they found out she'd been homeless, how would they react? And if word got out that she didn't have a high school diploma, it could hurt her business.

"My friends are nice," he said as if he could read her mind. "You don't have to worry about being judged or anything."

He was right. They were nice.

"Okay, I'll go." But she'd be careful not to reveal too much. The less they knew about her past, the better.

A few hours later, Mac wished he could stop looking Bridget's way. He shoved an empty pizza box in the trash as conversations buzzed around him. Some of his friends sat on the massive sectional, while others stood at the kitchen island near the open living space. Kaylee had gone over to Lydia's to spend the night, so it was only the adults—well, besides Holly's toddler, Clara, and Austin's baby, AJ. Tess and Sawyer had left little Tucker with her father.

Mac hadn't expected to see Bridget. Sure, he'd invited her, but she'd declined. Again. So when she'd arrived with Sawyer and Tess, he'd been surprised. And a little excited.

Bridget's straightforward what-you-see-is-what-you-get manner intrigued him, and she'd been a good influence on Kaylee. At the moment, she had a pleasant smile on her face as she held a can of soda and nodded at something Tess said.

The conversation around him kept circling back to Thanksgiving and Christmas. It would be Kaylee's first holiday season without their parents. He wanted to make it special for her. Give her a reason to not be sad. But he wasn't sure how.

"The calves doing okay?" Austin, popping a few peanuts into his mouth, came up to him. "Gaining weight?"

"Most are." He thought of the list of weaker ones and frowned. Every morning he checked on the calves he'd kept. Some were faring better than others. Was his dad right that keeping half of the calves to sell in the spring was a waste of time and money? "I'm supplementing their diets, but it's not doing much at this point for several of them."

"What kind of supplements?"

Mac explained the combination of tallow and fat blends as Austin nodded. While he spoke, he felt better about the decision to keep the calves. "I contacted an expert up in Montana. He told me what to do."

"Let me know how it goes. I might try keeping calves until spring, too, next year if it works out for you."

"I will." It was nice to hear something positive about his decision. Mac used to tell himself Dad wasn't a rancher and didn't have a clue what was best for the cattle, but more often than not, he forgot.

"Got the kitchen babyproofed last weekend." Austin grinned.

"Oh yeah?"

Mac spotted Austin's brother, Randy, carrying the baby. Hannah was glued to his side as she played peekaboo with the boy. Their engagement gave Mac a funny feeling. Not because he had a thing for Hannah or anything—he didn't— but because his world was changing. Some of the guys were falling in love. Getting engaged. Getting married.

Not him.

"Cassie insisted." Austin detailed how AJ's nanny supervised the childproofing of the house. "The cupboards weren't difficult…"

Mac peeked at Bridget again, now chuckling at something Blaine Mayer said. Blaine was a good guy. Another single rancher like him.

Bridget's chuckle turned into a guffaw, and Blaine grinned, leaning toward her.

Mac narrowed his eyes. Was Blaine flirting with Bridget?

His muscles tensed, and he excused himself to head in their direction.

"Oh, hey, Mac," Blaine said with a grin. "I was just telling Bridget about the time I took out a section of fence when Dad was teaching me how to drive."

They were sharing learning-to-drive stories. Harmless. He relaxed.

"Hey, Blaine, come over here, will you?" Jet called. Blaine excused himself, leaving Mac alone with Bridget. Her soft gray sweater skimmed her curves, and her slim-fitting dark pants were tucked into black boots. The silver necklace she wore seemed to be a staple of her wardrobe. He couldn't remember a time she wasn't wearing it.

Curious, he leaned in and lifted the charm to see it better.

"It's a sparrow." Her big brown eyes blinked up at him.

"Oh." He let the charm fall back into the hollow of her throat. "I like it."

"Thanks." She looked around. "You have a beautiful house."

"Thank you. My dad had it remodeled a few years ago."

"It's nice." Her gaze seemed to fall anywhere but him. "Did you pick everything out?"

"No." He swallowed the tang of copper in his mouth. Like his father would ever trust him with picking out furnishings for the home he lived in. "Dad had his own way of doing things. One day a contractor and interior designer showed up at my front door. They handled everything."

She studied him with a slight tilt of her head. "Would you have done anything differently?"

The question felt charged. He knew she meant with the house, but he couldn't help thinking about his father. Would he have done anything differently if Dad were still alive?

Yes. Mac probably should have stuck up for himself more. But where would it have gotten him? Kicked off the ranch, most likely.

"I like the house," he said. "I'm not really into decorating, but I wouldn't have minded being consulted about it."

Her expression softened. "I know what it's like to not have any say in your life." The words were so soft, he barely heard them.

He wasn't sure how to respond. He wanted to know more, though.

"Rough childhood?" His tone was light, but his gut clenched in preparation for her response.

"I survived." She shrugged. They stood there awkwardly for a few moments.

"How did you and Sawyer meet?" There. A safe topic of conversation.

A shadow crossed over her face. "Oh, out and about in the city."

Out and about? He didn't really care how they'd met, but he expected more details than that. "You kept bumping into each other or something?"

"We worked together."

"Makes sense." He got the distinct impression she wasn't being transparent.

"Joe says I need to decorate the store for Christmas." She took another sip of soda. "For an open house."

"Yeah, the open house is after the Christmas parade. You'll get a lot of business."

"I probably shouldn't expect the parade to be the same scale as Macy's, huh?" She set her soda can on a nearby table before giving him her full attention.

"Yeah, it's nothing like that." He chuckled. "The floats are all homemade. Each class from the high school makes one, and several local organizations put them together, too. There are fire trucks and people on horseback. Santa, of course. It's fun for the kids. I haven't been to it in years." He hadn't had any reason to attend. If he went this year, he'd probably get bombarded with requests to build a playground or donate money to help save endangered eagles or something.

He'd stopped taking Dina's calls, and he hadn't even glanced at the papers John Lutz had dropped off. Neither fact made him proud.

"Maybe I'll see if Kaylee could help me out that day." Bridget rubbed behind her ear. "Joe, too, if it's going to be busy."

"Nervous about him manning the store tomorrow?" Mac had been surprised when he found out she'd hired Joe Schlock for the Saturday mornings while she was in class. Joe was well-liked in these parts, but his lengthy conversations were merely tolerated by most people.

"Nervous? A little." She fingered the sparrow charm. "He knows how to make a good cup of coffee, though, and he's getting better on the register."

A *but* hung between them. He waited for her to expand. She didn't.

"I'm sure he'll be fine," Mac said. He fought the temptation to move closer to her. As it was, he was close enough to inhale her perfume, something fresh with a hint of vanilla.

"I hope so."

The air between them shimmered, and he couldn't look away from her lips. He shifted from one foot to the other. If he'd ever needed a distraction, now was the time.

Stop looking at her. Change the subject!

"It's Kaylee's first Thanksgiving here without our parents," he said quickly. "Christmas, too. I usually don't do a whole lot to celebrate. I want to make it special for her. Any suggestions?"

"No matter what you do, she's probably going to be sad."

That's what he was afraid of. "So, I shouldn't make big plans?"

"I didn't say that." Her rich brown eyes gleamed. "What does she normally do? What are her traditions?"

"I don't know." He winced and massaged the back of his neck.

"I guess you'll have to ask her."

"Yeah." Ask her. Why hadn't he thought of that? "Sometimes the most innocent topic makes her prickly."

"You can handle it." Her merry expression hit him in the best possible way. "After all, you're brave enough to teach the two of us how to drive."

He liked the word *brave*. He'd never felt particularly brave, though. Heat rushed up his neck.

"Speaking of driving, you need to get more hours behind the wheel. You can drive back to the coffee shop tomorrow after class."

"Do you think I'm ready?" Fear laced her tone.

"It's two miles. You'll be fine."

Her throat worked as she swallowed, causing the sparrow around her neck to fly. He couldn't stop staring at it or the pulse visibly fluttering in her neck.

"I'm glad you're confident about me driving." A shiver

shimmied her shoulders. "I feel like I'm a disaster waiting to happen."

"Nah, you're just new at it."

"Where did you get your patience?"

Not from my father.

"Hey, Mac, where do you keep your garbage bags?" Austin yelled. "I've got a nuclear diaper here…"

Tess and Sawyer approached as Mac excused himself and strode toward Austin. This was why he shouldn't be hanging out with Bridget. She kept looking at him more thoroughly than he was used to being viewed. And she'd zoomed to the heart of the matter when she'd let it slip that she knew what it was like to not have any say in her life.

Had a guy made her feel that way? The family she denied having?

What did it matter? He knew better than to explore more than friendship with her. But it didn't stop him from appreciating the peace of mind Bridget gave him in regard to Kaylee. She seemed to instinctively know what his sister needed in a way he didn't.

Yesterday nagged at him a little. Sometimes she pushed Kaylee too hard for his taste. So far, Kaylee was handling the pressure. If she started to crack, he'd step in and say something.

He wasn't letting anyone walk all over his little sister. And he wasn't letting anyone walk over himself, either.

"You're celebrating Thanksgiving with us," Tess said. Bridget tore her gaze away from where Mac stood laughing next to Austin. The man intrigued her more and more. Tess waved her finger. "We will not take no for an answer. Will we, Sawyer?"

"Nope." He had his arm slung over Tess's shoulders.

"Skip breakfast that morning, and prepare to be stuffed with turkey and pumpkin pie."

"Someone has to save me from eating half the pie by myself." Tess patted her tummy.

Bridget loved these two. Sawyer couldn't have found a better wife than Tess. She was funny, smart and had a huge heart.

"I'll pick you up," Sawyer said. "You can spend the night in the cabin if you'd like."

"Thank you. I'll sleep in my own bed." It was great to be included, but Bridget had her limits. "I'm finally getting more than three hours of sleep at night."

"See?" Tess said. "I knew you'd get used to the noises."

They discussed her driving class for a few minutes with Sawyer assuring her he'd take her driving whenever she wanted.

Then Jet called Sawyer over, and Holly took his place. Little Clara, adorable in a sweater with a pumpkin, striped leggings and an orange scrunchie headband, held her arms out to Bridget.

She blanked. Surely, the girl didn't want Bridget to hold her. She'd never held a child.

"Oh, Clara, don't you want Aunt Tess to hold you?" Tess reached for her, but Clara only had eyes for Bridget.

"I'm sorry. She seems to really like you." Holly looked embarrassed as Clara bounced on her hip for Bridget to take her.

There was nothing to do but pick the child up. Bridget took the girl in her arms and held her on her hip. A wave of delight rushed over her as Clara snuggled into her side. She smelled fresh in the way only a baby could.

"How old is she?"

"Just turned one." Holly adjusted Clara's shirt. "She's growing up too fast."

Bridget glanced up and saw Mac across the room. The intense gleam in his eyes made her flush. What was it about him that drew her so?

"I think it's super nice of you to hire Joe." Hannah joined the group.

She'd been into the coffee shop several afternoons with her service-dog-in-training, Barley. Apparently, she was raising the puppy for the next year with the hopes he'd be chosen to continue on as a service dog. The golden retriever was not only adorable, but well-behaved, too. He was spending quality time with Hannah's parents tonight. Randy's service dog, Ned, was here to alert him of any symptoms related to his heart condition.

"Well, I'm grateful to have him help out for the next couple of weeks." Hearing Joe's name brought a fresh case of nerves. Bridget still wasn't sure how customers would respond to him. She really needed those Saturday sales.

"He'll talk your ear off, that's for sure, but he'll also drop anything to help you." Hannah smiled. "He's a social kind of guy."

"Joe is the nicest man." Tess splayed her hands near her chest. "But don't think I haven't hustled in the other direction if I'm in a hurry. I don't have time for his rambling stories."

Bridget had the feeling a lot of other people around town felt that way, too. The ladies who'd snubbed him last week, for sure. If her regulars knew Joe was going to be in charge of Brewed Awakening on Saturdays, they might avoid the place.

Well, so be it. If she hadn't hired him, the coffee shop would be locked until tomorrow afternoon. Was that any better?

Clara, with her mouth wide open, grabbed the sparrow on her necklace.

"No, no, baby." Holly gently took her hand away from it, then met Bridget's eyes. "She'll yank it right off your neck if you aren't careful."

"Thanks for the warning." The necklace meant a lot to her. She'd purchased it after getting baptized several years ago. It reminded her that she was more important to God even than sparrows, and the thought always gave her peace.

She'd felt less important than a sparrow many times in her life. That God loved her so much was humbling.

"So, be honest," Hannah said. Bridget tensed. Honest? About what? "Are you bored out of your mind yet? I mean Sunrise Bend is night and day from New York City."

She exhaled in relief. This was a topic she didn't need to avoid.

"Oh, no. I'm not bored. I do miss the shopping, though. When I get my license, I'm driving to the nearest Target and going wild."

The ladies laughed, and Clara giggled, too. Bridget held her tighter. Precious little thing.

"We might have to make a weekend of it," Hannah said. "The nearest one is hours away, and I love going wild in Target."

"Who's going wild where?" Randy sidled up next to Hannah, slipping his arm around her waist. The black Lab stayed by his side.

"We're all going wild." Hannah grinned up at him. "Christmas is right around the corner. We need to have a party."

The other guys joined the circle.

"Can't we get through Thanksgiving first? And no parties." Blaine pretended to gag. "Isn't this party enough?"

"You're scared we'll invite Janelle or Maggie," Tess said, high-fiving Holly.

"Don't even threaten me with those two." Blaine looked dead serious.

"Relax." Holly's eyes twinkled. "We know you're not looking for a girlfriend."

"Got that right." Blaine put his arm around Mac's neck. "No matchmaking, you two. I'm not looking. Neither is Mac. Or Austin. We're free, aren't we, boys?"

Bridget couldn't look away from Mac, and it hit her that he wasn't looking away from her either.

Single. Free.

She was the same. She'd never allowed herself to dream otherwise. But now? She touched the sparrow charm and watched Mac.

Maybe single didn't always mean being free. She looked around this group of friends and acknowledged something had shifted in her tonight.

She'd love to have what they had. However, Blaine and Mac and Austin were single by choice. She wasn't. And that wasn't going to change.

Chapter Six

"Try to park between the lines."

Bridget ignored her galloping pulse as she attempted to guide Mac's truck into a diagonal parking spot near Brewed Awakening. She inched it forward. *Brake. Accelerate. Brake. Accelerate.* It stopped with a jerk.

She never wanted to drive again.

Kaylee hopped out of the back seat, came around the front of the truck, stood on the sidewalk and gave her two thumbs-up. "You're only over the line a little bit."

"I don't think I'm supposed to be over it at all." Bridget climbed out and checked the lines. Kaylee was correct. She had crossed it slightly.

The urge to run into the shop and forget the previous ten minutes of her life hit her hard. Driving on the actual road had been frightening. It had only compounded her already high anxiety about leaving Joe alone at the shop. All throughout the class her mind had wandered.

Had Joe scared off her customers?

Had she even had any customers?

"Hop in, Kay. Your turn." Mac stood on the sidewalk not far from Bridget and pointed to the truck door.

Why was the man so calm? And so handsome? Whenever she looked at his face, she'd find herself staring. It was like being sucked into a force field. Maybe she'd be better off never looking his way again. Fat chance of that happening.

"I'm not ready." Kaylee shook her head, the color leaching from her cheeks. "I'll do it later."

The girl's reluctance was justified—Bridget had given herself the mother of all internal pep talks only ten minutes prior—but Kaylee would miss out on life if she never challenged herself.

Bridget half expected Mac to insist she drive, but then, he was a softy where Kaylee was concerned. He'd let her slink away without putting up a fight. He didn't seem to get that his sister's insecurity would only get worse if she didn't face her fears.

"You did good the other day," he said.

Huh. Maybe he would insist after all.

"That was in the parking lot. This is the *road*." Kaylee opened her eyes wide for emphasis.

Bridget pinpointed the exact moment he caved.

"All right, but you have to get used to driving or what's the point of getting your license?"

"I will." She smiled, rushing to him and giving him a hug.

"Thanks for the ride." Bridget waved to them both. She'd interfered last time in the church parking lot, and she regretted it. Meddling didn't come naturally to her, and that was how she wanted to keep it. "And thanks for the lesson."

"You're welcome." Mac hitched his chin to her. She studied the pair for a moment as they got back into the truck and drove away. Then she shook her thoughts free and walked into the coffee shop. *Please let there be customers inside.*

As soon as she entered, she braced herself for the worst—an empty store. To her surprise all the tables were filled but one, and there were only two seats left at the counter. Joe stood near the register as he wiped a mug with a towel and chatted with an older man she didn't recognize.

"Ah, there she is." Joe beamed when he spotted her. "Like I was telling you, Simon, Bridget's got a knack for running this place. Makes a dynamite cup of coffee, too."

The strangest sensation spilled down her gut. Joe acted as if he were proud of her. Like a father would be. Like her own father never had been.

She swallowed the sudden emotions in her throat, gave them both a weak smile and fled to the back. After tying on her apron, she took a few deep breaths. Part of her plan to keep a low profile in Sunrise Bend required a certain detachment. Joe's blind faith in her was leaving her decidedly undetached.

And that could hurt her.

She emerged from the back room and took her spot behind the counter.

"How did it go today?" she asked Joe.

"Good." His good nature had clearly soared to new heights based on his expression. "Well, the register and I had a spat, but we worked it out."

"Yeah, after you scared Janet away." Simon, the wiry, bald man Joe had been talking to, let out a throaty laugh. His wrinkled face was weathered from years in the sun. Addressing Bridget, Simon pointed to Joe. "This one talks too much."

"No one scared anyone away." Joe scowled. "Don't listen to him. He's sore because he missed out on the last pumpkin muffin."

"If you wouldn't have been jabbing at the machine so

hard, you might have realized you were down to one muffin and saved it for me."

"The pumpkin muffins sold out?" Bridget couldn't believe it. She'd baked two dozen last night after coming home from Mac's house, and on a whim, she'd smeared on cream cheese frosting. Five of them had not been lookers. Okay, six. She'd priced them all low.

"Yep. Lots of compliments on them, too." There was that gleam of pride in his eyes again.

"Any problems?" What had Simon meant about scaring Janet away and Joe jabbing at the machine so hard?

"Well, if you count Janet pointedly asking him if he only worked on Saturdays, then yeah, you might have a problem." Simon's cloudy gray eyes twinkled. He was clearly enjoying tattling on Joe. "She wants to avoid him."

"She'll come back." Joe waved off the statement. "Where else can she go for a toasted butterscotch macchiato? The Barking Squirrel has two types of coffee— regular and decaf. Period."

Bridget debated asking if this Janet planned on spreading the word about not coming in when he was there. But Joe looked so happy in his apron, drying her mugs, she didn't have the heart to say anything.

"What's your story, girlie?" Simon gestured to her and took another sip from his mug.

"Story?" She'd been getting these questions for days. "Not much to tell."

"Is that so?" He arched his eyebrows in skepticism, still holding the mug. "A pretty thing like you moving to a nowhere town like this? Doesn't pass the smell test. And I've heard you've been tight-lipped with everyone when asked about it."

"You think I'm pretty?" She pretended to laugh. Best

to latch on to something easy. Maybe he'd let go of the rumor about her being tight-lipped.

"False modesty won't work with me. A gal like you can take your pick of any of the young bucks around here, and you know it." He grinned, then downed the final swig of his coffee.

She didn't know it, but it was nice of him to say.

"Leave her alone, you old bag of nails." Joe held the coffee pot up, and at Simon's nod, refilled his mug. He placed the pot back on the warmer and addressed Bridget. "Ignore him. We're glad you moved here. Sunrise Bend is a good place to live."

"I agree." She bent down to grab the stack of receipts from the shelf below the register. "Thanks again for helping me out. You can go ahead and take off…"

"I can stay for a while. I'll clean off that table." He took a cloth and bottle of spray over to the vacated table.

She flipped through the receipts, scanning them while Simon drank in silence.

Sales had been good. Really good.

A young family with a small boy and a baby entered. Bridget shoved the receipts back under the counter and gave them a pleasant smile.

"Welcome to Brewed Awakening," she said: "What can I get you?"

The brunette hiked the baby higher on her hip. A little girl from the looks of it. Reminded Bridget of how Clara had felt in her arms last night. What an unexpected pleasure that had been.

"Stay here." The young father grabbed the boy's hood before he could run off. Then he turned up his nose at the menu. "Don't you got something plain? I don't go for fancy."

"Of course. We have regular coffee in a dark roast and a blond roast. Decaf, too. Our flavor of the day is pecan brittle."

"I don't know." The woman bit her lower lip and glanced at her husband. "Maybe we should go."

He didn't need to be told twice. He herded the boy toward the door with his wife scurrying behind him. "Riley was right. These prices are outrageous."

Bridget bristled. Outrageous? Her prices were lower than most nationwide chains.

"Don't mind them." Simon shook his head. "They're frugal folk. When Marge and Bud owned this place, they charged about the same as you. Their daughter Riley actually raised prices when she took it over."

Bridget did *not* have a good attitude about Riley Sampson. She had been pitting the town against Brewed Awakening before it even opened. Couldn't the woman let it go?

"People are curious about you." He stared over the rim. "The curiosity brings them in. But what will keep them coming back is your coffee. Joe's right. Best I've had."

Unexpected emotion pressed against her chest. What a kind thing to say. "Thank you, Simon. What's your last name?"

"Valentine."

"Really?"

"Yep. My favorite holiday is Valentine's Day, too. Got it named after me and everything." He rose, tossing a few ones on the counter. "Nice to meet you, Bridget."

"My last name's Renna."

"I know that, too. Everyone around here does. See you around." Then he turned to walk out, lifting a hand in farewell. "Bye, Joe."

Joe returned and stashed the cleaning supplies. "I'm telling you, this place needs Christmas decorations. I have lots of ornaments in my attic if you need them. They've been up there for a couple of decades, so they might be dusty. Probably smell of mothballs, now that I think of it.

Hope there aren't any mice. Hmm…we stored some decorations for Linda's friend, but she died and…"

"That's okay." Bridget was tempted to take him up on the offer, though. She'd been a thrift shopper for years, and the only thing better than cheap was free. But old, smelly decorations from his attic wouldn't lure in customers. Mice wouldn't either. "I'll buy some soon. I have to make everything fit into my theme."

"Theme?" He scratched his chin. "What do you mean?"

"The coffee shop I worked for in the city always had a Christmas theme. I need the mood in here to be just right."

"Well, you know what you're doing. Me, I unravel the ball of lights and string 'em up here and there and all over. Except the porch. Boy, that was a mistake. It happened a few years ago, or was it last winter? No, it was the year before. Anyway, the wind tore the lights down…"

As he continued on about lights flying into the ditch and a Christmas tree topper stuck against his porch rail, Bridget surveyed the coffee shop, trying to decide what color scheme to go with. It depended on if she wanted it to look elegant. Or bright and cheery. Or kid-friendly. Or rustic-chic.

"…and I tell you it's strange to see a tree with colored lights on top and white ones on the bottom. Don't know why Sheryl thought mixing the two would work…" Joe kept talking.

She took out her cell phone and texted Sawyer.

What are you doing after church tomorrow?

A few seconds ticked by before he replied.

Ken's not feeling well. Tess is taking care of him, so I might not make it tomorrow. His oncologist appointment is next week. Hope it's nothing. Would you mind praying for him?

That didn't sound good. According to Sawyer, Tess's father had been managing his lung cancer pretty well all year. She hated to think he might be getting worse.

She typed, Of course. Please tell Tess I'm praying.

Bridget sighed. There went her plan to shop for decorations tomorrow.

A ding had her checking the phone again. Sawyer replied Do you need me to take you somewhere?

She would not ask that of him. No. Stay with Tess.

Bridget lightly bit her lower lip as she debated what to do. She did have someone else she could ask. She was relying on Mac too much, though. It wasn't as if she had much choice. She had to rely on someone until she got her license.

Decision made. She'd call Mac later. Maybe he'd be willing to give her and Kaylee another driving lesson tomorrow…all the way to the store where she could buy some decorations.

Relying on other people wasn't her strong suit. And she'd had to do that again and again since moving here.

She thought of Mac, of Kaylee, of Sawyer and Tess. Maybe relying on others wasn't the end of the world. Still…she craved independence. And Mac's driving lessons would give her just that.

Sunday afternoon Mac gripped the handle above the window as Bridget merged onto the highway. He'd been keyed up to get her call last night, even if it had been to request a driving lesson to the nearest shopping center. He'd figured Bridget could get a good hour of practice in on the way there, and Kaylee could drive on the way back.

His sister, however, had other plans. She never had other plans.

Kaylee was spending the day at the high school helping

plan the decorations for the parade floats each class would be building. It was the first time she'd gotten involved with anything school-related.

Maybe he should have stayed home…just in case Kaylee needed him.

The truck swerved. He squeezed the handle tightly.

"Am I doing this right?" Bridget had both hands on the wheel in a death grip, and she was leaning forward like an old lady in a cartoon.

"You're going too slow. You want to stay close to the speed limit." Mac was glad there weren't many vehicles on the road today.

"The speed limit? That's way too fast." Her forehead wrinkled with worry.

"It will feel natural—don't sweat it." He let go of the handle and tapped his fingertips on his thighs. "You look uncomfortable. Why don't you relax into the seat?"

"Then I won't be able to see the road." She flicked a scared look his way.

"You'll be able to see it." Maybe this would be easier for her if he took her mind off her fears. "How did Joe do yesterday?"

"Pretty good, considering." Her gaze was locked ahead, but she relaxed a bit.

"Considering what?"

"Well, he's new to my computer system. And he's chatty."

"Yeah, he is." Mac chuckled. "He talks Randy's ear off every afternoon at his store."

"I don't mind. But…some of the customers might."

"Anyone specific?"

"Some of the middle-aged and older ladies. A Janet in particular."

"Ahh. Janet Jones. Dina's mother-in-law. She's a nice woman. Strong opinions. Gets things done."

"Hmm." Her shoulders finally rested against the back of the seat. "Maybe that's why he annoys her. She has things to do, and his rambling holds her up."

"I wouldn't be surprised." Mac thought of his father and how he'd rudely cut someone off if they interfered with his schedule, but the man would talk for hours to someone he wanted to partner with. "My dad could be like that, too."

"Do you miss him?"

Did he? They hadn't been close. They'd talked once a month or so, but it was usually to go over ranch numbers.

"Sometimes." It was true. Dad had a larger-than-life presence, but he also had a good sense of humor and occasionally had confided things Mac had never expected him to share. Those were the times Mac yearned for. When his father had treated him like an equal. "Do you miss yours?"

"Sometimes." She glanced at him then, and his stomach flip-flopped. "He was great about some things…and not so great about others."

"Same as mine." He found himself wanting to talk about his father for once. "My dad had a tendency to steamroll everyone. He wasn't a jerk. It was more like determination. Ambition. What he wanted, he got, and if you didn't agree, you were wrong."

"Did you ever disagree with him?"

"Oh, yeah. Just not to his face, unless it was really important."

"Like what?" She kept a steady speed and seemed less scared.

"How to run the ranch." Mac clenched his jaw. Last year he'd decided a phone call wouldn't cut it with Dad, so he'd flown to Texas to discuss his plans on keeping half the calves. Had prepared a presentation with charts and graphs and everything. Dad had barely paid attention and dismissed his ideas as dumb.

Just thinking about it made Mac feel like an idiot all over again.

"I thought you owned the ranch." She kept her gaze straight ahead as they continued on a flat stretch of highway.

"I do now. But when Dad was alive, he never signed it over to me. I went to Texas last summer to convince him to try something new. I never should have gone. He liked having his hands in my business too much. Liked having something to threaten me with."

"He threatened you?"

He shouldn't have said so much. "More like leverage to get his way. Forget it. It's hard to explain."

"Emotional blackmail," she said under her breath. "My stepmother was an expert at it. And my dad let her walk all over him."

Let her walk all over him... He knew those words well, and they never ceased to bother him. "You keep in touch with her?"

"No." The word was curt.

"Start easing off the gas." He pointed to the curve up ahead. "See the sign? That's how fast you should go when you take the turn."

"What happens after the turn?"

"You speed back up." He grinned at her as she concentrated as if her life depended on it. "You're doing good. I wish Kaylee would get a good chunk of practice in like this."

"She'll want to once she gets more comfortable behind the wheel."

"Yeah, but how do I get her behind the wheel? She's too scared to try."

"You seem to know when she needs patience or when she needs a push."

Did he know? He'd always loved Kaylee, but he'd never lived with her. The two weeks in the summers didn't count. And besides cattle, he didn't push anything. Why would he?

His phone rang. Was something wrong with Kaylee? His heart started beating rapidly. He checked the caller and rolled his eyes. Dina Jones.

"You can take it," Bridget said. "I don't mind."

"No. It's not important. Just another request for money to help out the booster club."

"Another request?"

He kept his tone light as he filled her in on all the requests he'd gotten over the past months.

"That's awful. They shouldn't be hitting you up for money. I don't care how much you inherited."

She clearly had no idea how much he inherited or she wouldn't feel that way.

"No big deal," he said, wanting to change the subject. "What are you shopping for today?"

"Christmas decorations for the store." She bit her lower lip. "For my apartment, too, I suppose."

They discussed artificial versus real trees and whether white lights were better than multicolored, and soon he was directing her to their exit. A few minutes later, she successfully parked in a vacant area at the far end of the lot.

"Nice job," he said as he got out.

"Thanks." She drew her shoulders up to her ears at the chill in the air, and her pretty face lost the pinched look from earlier. He couldn't help but stare. "I feel a little better about driving now. Getting on the highway was scary, but once I merged, it wasn't so bad. Would you mind if I drove home, too?"

"You should." They began walking to the main entrance. "If you keep practicing like this, once you're done with driver's ed classes you can get your license right away."

"You think so?" They kept an easy pace across the lot. "*If* I can keep practicing. I feel bad asking you to give up your free time."

"It's what friends do." He shot her a confused glance. "I'm your friend, right?"

"Yes." Her eyelashes dipped. "You are."

They were friends. Driving together. Shopping together. The closer they got, the more he revealed to her.

What would happen if he let the truth slip out? He'd never lived up to his dad's expectations and didn't deserve the ranch or the inheritance.

She'd think he was a pushover. She'd walk all over him.

He shouldn't be giving her mixed signals—and he shouldn't be giving himself mixed signals either. What he was feeling was more than friendship. And he didn't need any more friends.

Had she bitten off more than she could chew with a seven-foot tree? Later that evening Bridget was overloaded with shopping bags as she attempted to insert her key into the apartment door's lock. In the city she'd simply set up a two-foot-tall pre-lit tree and pop a few candy canes and tinsel on it. There hadn't been room in her tiny apartment for anything else. Now that she had the space, she'd gone a little overboard with the decorations she'd purchased with Mac.

"Here, let me." Mac took the key from her hand and unlocked the door swiftly. Then he opened it and followed her inside with the large tree box hefted on his shoulder.

Today had been fun. And scary. But mostly fun.

She flicked on the lights and let the bags drop to the

floor. Driving wasn't as terrifying as it had been yesterday. Dare she say she was actually getting the hang of it? Mostly because of Mac. He'd been blessed with an extra helping of patience.

And she'd enjoyed his company all day. He was easy to be with. At the store, they'd loaded two carts with inexpensive bulbs, lights, artificial greenery, wreaths and two artificial Christmas trees. One for her apartment and one for the coffee shop. He'd picked up some items he thought Kaylee might like, then they'd stopped at an Italian restaurant for a bite to eat.

On the way home, she'd felt more comfortable driving and had asked him about the ranch and what he did there. After hearing the details of raising cattle, she was even more glad she worked inside making coffee. His life sounded like a lot of hard, physical work. And he did it in all kinds of weather. He had to make tough choices, too, which she didn't envy.

"Where do you want this?" He kept one hand on the tree box propped vertically next to him.

"Oh, anywhere." She doubted she'd be doing anything with it for a few weeks. She had too much to think about already. Once she got her driver's license, she'd have more time on her hands. Room to breathe again. Then she'd figure out Christmas.

Her traditions consisted of watching a movie in her apartment with a cup of hot cocoa when her shift ended on Christmas Eve. She always worked Christmas Day, too. Then she and Sawyer would get together the day after Christmas and share a pizza and a small gift. It had been fine—a step up from the holidays after her father died—until last year when Sawyer moved back to Wyoming.

It was at that point she'd realized how alone she really was. The cup of cocoa and movie hadn't cut it, and the video call with Sawyer the day after Christmas hadn't either.

"Is over here okay?" Mac was already carrying it to the far corner of the living room where she'd set a used end table.

"Sure."

"I like what you've done with the place." Mac was giving the room a once-over. She'd only had two people up so far—Sawyer and Tess. It was strange having Mac up here, too. Yet, he looked like he belonged. To be honest, no matter where he was, he looked like he belonged. He just had a kind of air about him.

She'd never belonged. She was achingly aware of it even if she'd learned to keep it hidden well. Bridget would like to belong in Sunrise Bend, but she didn't know if it was possible.

"Yeah, it's eclectic." Her furniture was a mishmash of secondhand finds she'd picked up over the years.

"It's you." He met her eyes and smiled, cueing her pulse to take off. "You picked out everything, right?"

"I did." Would she have selected the same if she could have afforded more? She didn't know. The apartment was starting to feel comfortable. That was all that mattered. She remembered Mac saying his house had been professionally decorated. It made her feel better. His house was comfortable, too.

She was getting more and more curious about Mac. Like what he'd shared about his father on the ride.

"The talk you had with your father last year to try something new—what was it?" Bridget gestured for him to sit on the oversize chair while she took a seat on her worn, sage green sofa. He obliged.

"You want to know about my idea for the ranch?" He spread his knees and let his elbows rest on them.

"Well, yeah."

"I wanted to sell half the calves in the fall. Keep the others to fatten up and sell in the spring. He thought it was a stupid idea."

"Why?" She knew nothing about ranching beyond what Sawyer had told her of his childhood and what Mac had shared about his daily life.

"It costs money to feed them all winter, plus the weather gets harsh around here. There's less chance of them thriving during the cold months. We usually sell all the calves in the fall, and the sales carry us over financially until spring."

"Oh. I didn't realize."

"Now that Dad's not here to stop me, I did things my way. This year will be tight, profit-wise, since I'm using the ranch's reserve funds to get through the winter, but once spring comes around, we should have a good handle on what we need to do to stay profitable moving forward."

Reserve funds. She knew all about those. It had taken her four years to build the tiniest of nest eggs. Four more to grow it to a cushion that kept her from panicking every day about losing her job. It had taken two more years to save what had ended up being the down payment for this business.

Even with her reserves, she worried about losing it all.

She had the feeling she'd always worry. Being homeless for almost two months tended to do that to a person.

But Mac had an inheritance. One big enough that people around town expected him to donate to their causes.

"It must be a relief to finally run the ranch your way. And you could always dip into your inheritance if money gets tight."

"That's Dad's money."

FREE BOOKS GIVEAWAY

2 FREE ROMANCE BOOKS!

2 FREE SUSPENSE BOOKS!

GET UP TO FOUR FREE BOOKS & TWO FREE GIFTS WORTH OVER $20!

We pay for everything!

YOU pick your books –
WE pay for everything.
You get up to FOUR New Books and TWOMystery Gifts...absolutely FREE!

Dear Reader,

I am writing to announce the launch of a huge **FREE BOOKS GIVEAWAY**... and to let you know that YOU are entitled to choose up to FOUR fantastic books that WE pay for.

Try **Love Inspired® Romance Larger-Print** books and fall in love with inspirational romances that take you on an uplifting journey of faith, forgiveness and hope.

Try **Love Inspired® Suspense Larger-Print** books where courage and optimism unite in stories of faith and love in the face of danger.

Or TRY BOTH!

In return, we ask just one favor: Would you please participate in our brief Reader Survey? We'd love to hear from you.

This FREE BOOKS GIVEAWAY means that your introductory shipment is completely free, <u>even the shipping</u>! If you decide to continue, you can look forward to curated monthly shipments of brand-new books from your selected series, always at a discount off the cover price! <u>Plus you can cancel any time</u>. Who could pass up a deal like that?

Sincerely

Pam Powers

Pam Powers
For Harlequin Reader Service

Complete the survey below and return it today to receive up to 4 FREE BOOKS and FREE GIFTS guaranteed!

FREE BOOKS GIVEAWAY
Reader Survey

1

Do you prefer books which reflect Christian values?

◯ YES ◯ NO

2

Do you share your favorite books with friends?

◯ YES ◯ NO

3

Do you often choose to read instead of watching TV?

◯ YES ◯ NO

YES! Please send me my Free Rewards, consisting of **2 Free Books** from each series I select and **Free Mystery Gifts**. I understand that I am under no obligation to buy anything, no purchase necessary see terms and conditions for details.

❑ **Love Inspired® Romance Larger-Print** (122/322 IDL GRP7)
❑ **Love Inspired® Suspense Larger-Print** (107/307 IDL GRP7)
❑ **Try Both** (122/322 & 107/307 IDL GRQK)

FIRST NAME

LAST NAME

ADDRESS

APT.#

CITY

STATE/PROV.

ZIP/POSTAL CODE

EMAIL ❑ Please check this box if you would like to receive newsletters and promotional emails from Harlequin Enterprises ULC and its affiliates. You can unsubscribe anytime.

If offer card is missing write to: Harlequin Reader Service, P.O. Box 1341, Buffalo, NY 14240-8531 or visit www.ReaderService.com

BUSINESS REPLY MAIL
FIRST-CLASS MAIL   PERMIT NO. 717   BUFFALO, NY

POSTAGE WILL BE PAID BY ADDRESSEE

HARLEQUIN READER SERVICE
PO BOX 1341
BUFFALO NY 14240-8571

NO POSTAGE
NECESSARY
IF MAILED
IN THE
UNITED STATES

Was that how he saw it? Maybe he wanted nothing to do with the inheritance.

"Yours now," she said.

"You're right," he said. "It's good to finally do things my way. But with Dad's death, there are other things I have to make decisions about, and I never wanted to make them. Still don't want to. Makes my life more complicated."

"Are you talking about Kaylee?"

"No, she's—I'd do anything for her. She's all I've got left." The honesty in his eyes convinced her of what she already knew. He'd never consider Kaylee to be a chore or a complication.

"These other decisions..." She tried to find the right words, not sure what they were talking about. "You'll get them figured out."

Surprise flashed across his face, followed by a look of resignation. "I hope you're right."

"I am."

"Well, I should probably get going." He rose, his gaze resting on her for a long moment.

"I really appreciate all you've done for me, Mac." Saying his name sent a tingle across her skin. "You're giving me my freedom. Teaching me to drive."

"Freedom?" He started walking toward the door, and she followed him. "You're as free as anyone I know."

"Me? Why do you say that?"

He reached for the handle. "You make all the decisions for yourself, and, from what you told me, you don't owe anyone a thing."

She supposed it was true. "I'll owe you rent soon."

His gaze smoldered. "You know what I mean. You don't have to answer to anyone."

Her heart sank. Yes, she liked making her own decisions. No, she didn't owe anyone anything besides the rent. But not having anyone to answer to wasn't always a good thing.

Because no one needed her.

She wished she had a family to answer to, who wanted her around on holidays. Parents who would have made sure she had enough to eat and a place to live.

Being independent was a double-edged sword.

Mac gave her a final, lingering look before leaving. She shut the door and locked it, turning to lean against it.

Why would Mac—who had security, friends, money— consider her to have more freedom than he did? It was a quandary she doubted she'd get to the bottom of any-time soon.

Chapter Seven

❧

Two weeks later, Thanksgiving arrived cold and overcast. Bridget was driving Sawyer's truck with him next to her in the passenger seat. Her nerves were on the jittery side, not because of driving, but because she'd never spent Thanksgiving with a normal family before. She didn't know what to expect. The holidays had always been for other people to enjoy.

At least it would be an intimate affair. Just Sawyer, Tess, Ken and little Tucker at their ranch. Bridget got along well with all of them.

"I'm sorry I haven't been able to get you out driving this week." Sawyer flashed a contrite look her way. "With Ken's chemo starting back up, I've been on daddy duty more. It would be a big help to have a cancer center closer by. The drive's getting to Tess."

"How far away is it?" She'd never really thought about the medical facilities in a small town. She rarely got sick, and when she did, a few days in bed typically got her back on her feet.

"Over an hour."

"I'm sorry. That must be hard on all of you."

"It's toughest on Tess. Ken never complains about his

treatments, but when he's miserable, he bosses her around. Then those two go at it. And ten minutes later they're hugging like they never fought."

"Really?" She peeked at Sawyer. "Is that normal?"

"It is for them." He grinned. "I'm used to it. It's been that way since I met them. By the way, Tess invited a few more people over for supper. She's been trying to get her ex's family more involved with Tucker. Hope that's okay."

The hair on the back of her neck rose. *I thought you said it was going to be just us? I thought you said it would be small and low-key?*

The thoughts mortified her. Who was she to tell Sawyer who to invite to his own home? "It's good for Tucker to have them around."

"I don't know if they're coming or not."

She hoped not. A blast of guilt slapped her for being so selfish.

"How did driver's ed go this week?"

"It's as boring as ever. And don't take my word for it. Kaylee agrees." Bridget flashed him a grin. "The instructor's been having us drive, so that helps. Plus, Mac has been taking me and Kaylee out quite a bit."

The three of them were becoming fast friends—talking about their days, enjoying each other's company—but she had a terrible feeling that as soon as she got her license, the friendship would fade.

She'd been doing a rotten job of protecting her heart.

At least she'd kept her promise to keep her past in the past. She'd only opened up to Mac about innocent things, memories that wouldn't change the way he viewed her. But the fact remained she was getting too close to him and his sister.

"Start slowing down. The turn's up ahead."

Bridget eased her foot off the gas, carefully applied

the brake and made a right turn down the winding drive to the ranch.

"Nice job. That was smooth," he said. "When will you be done? Saturday? Or next week?"

"Saturday. If I pass the test, I can technically go to the DMV and get my license."

"I'll take you if you want."

"Thanks, Sawyer." She slowed as the house came into view. No vehicles other than Tess's and Ken's were there. *Phew.*

Would it really be so bad to have Thanksgiving with people other than Sawyer's family?

Yes.

Because she didn't know how these holiday celebrations worked. And being around strangers meant more small talk. She didn't mind small talk at the coffee shop, but off duty? No, thanks.

They both got out of the truck, and Bridget shivered at how cold it was outside. A gust of wind flattened her hair against her neck. She hurried next to Sawyer up the porch to the door where a pretty wreath wrapped in plaid ribbon hung. Inside, they toed off their boots, hung up their coats and made their way down the hall to the kitchen where Tucker was begging Tess for more juice.

"You already had juice. Here's some water." She handed the boy—recently turned three—a sippy cup. He threw it on the ground and stamped his feet. "Young man, you do not want a time-out. Pick that back up."

Sawyer kissed Tess's cheek. Bridget loved seeing their tender affection for each other. It was so foreign from what she'd been around as a kid. She crouched to greet Tucker. "Hey, Tuck, I brought you something."

His demeanor went from sullen to jubilant in a split-second. "Aunt Bwidget!"

"I figured you needed another one." She pulled a small toy tractor from her tote and handed it to him.

"A twactor!" He threw his arms around her, then raced off to the living room with it in his chubby little hand. "Papa, look!"

Bridget took a package of dinner rolls out of her tote and handed them to Tess.

"You didn't have to bring anything." Tess pulled her in for a hug.

"I wanted to. They're not homemade, sorry."

"I've never baked homemade rolls in my life." Tess seemed proud of the fact. "The freezer section at the supermarket is my best friend."

Someone knocked at the front door. Tess pointed to Sawyer. "Will you let them in?"

Bridget's stomach plunged. There went her hope for an intimate dinner. She tried to mentally prepare herself for strangers and polite chitchat. *God, this isn't my thing. I shouldn't have come. I don't even have a car or I could make an excuse and leave.*

Well, that wasn't her best prayer. But the church she'd attended in the city had emphasized that you could pray to God about anything, and she'd taken their word for it.

Voices grew closer. She recognized them. The higher-pitched one belonged to Kaylee. The lower? Mac.

Her heart began to pound. What was worse—Thanksgiving with strangers or Thanksgiving with the man she thought about night and day? The one she admired more and more?

"Happy Thanksgiving, Bridget!" Kaylee hugged her. "I knew you'd be here. Can you believe Mac made no plans for Thanksgiving? He was going to order food for the two of us. I was like, uh, no. Not when we could hang out here with you guys."

Bridget was amazed this was the same nervous, with-drawn girl she'd met only a month ago. Kaylee was clearly blossoming, and Bridget was happy to see it.

"I'm glad we can all celebrate together." Bridget gave her a quick hug. She meant it, too.

"Hi, Bridget." Mac nodded to her.

"Hey." She got lost in his eyes—dark gray and as tur-bulent as a storm brewing. He shifted from one foot to the other, clearly uncomfortable. That made two of them. She blurted out the first thing that came to mind. "Happy Thanksgiving."

"Same to you." He nodded. "Hope you don't mind us crashing the party."

"It's not crashing when you're invited." Tess playfully smacked his upper arm. "Come on, you guys can help me move the food to the table. We're about ready to eat."

They all grabbed platters and serving dishes on their way to the dining room, where the table was set with a pretty autumn-themed tablecloth and individual place set-tings of fine china.

"Just find the little card with your name on it." Tess waved to the table.

"This is so fancy." Bridget couldn't help but be delighted at the handwritten cards set on top of the plates. So this was what a real Thanksgiving dinner looked like.

"We only use Mom's good plates a few times a year," Tess said. "It makes me happy when I see them."

Mom's good plates. Bridget had nothing of her moth-er's. Nothing of her father's, either.

"Looks like you're here." Mac pulled the chair out for Bridget. She glanced up to thank him and was surprised to see the muscle in his cheek flexing. The man seemed edgy about something.

"Is anything wrong?" she asked quietly.

His face went slack before he gave her a tight smile. "No. Everything's fine."

He was lying. But why?

Why would Mac be upset? Did he not want to be here? Or maybe he didn't want her to be here. She had no clue.

As soon as Ken, on the pale side, sat at the head of the table and Sawyer took his place at the other end, Ken said a heartfelt prayer. Then Tess announced it was time to dig in.

Turkey was passed around, and Bridget overloaded her plate with extra-large helpings of mashed potatoes and stuffing. There was something about carbs. Mmm-mmm. Chitchat traveled around the table with Bridget listening to everything being said, content to take it in and not contribute.

They discussed the weather, how the cattle were doing on both ranches, Tucker's progress recognizing the alphabet and Kaylee's efforts at helping make her class's float for the upcoming Christmas parade. Then the attention zoomed to Bridget.

"How is business?" Tess asked. "Is Saturday Joe's last day?"

"Yes." And Bridget was kind of on the fence about it.

"Well, that will make some of the ladies around town happy." Tess went on to mention a few of the comments she'd heard when checking in with her bookkeeping clients.

"He's doing a good job." Bridget tried not to bristle at the comments. The man was the ideal employee. He worked hard, made excellent coffee and never complained.

"Oh, I know he is." Tess gave her a sympathetic look. "It wasn't as if you had much choice. You needed someone to take care of the shop while you were gone. And, between you and me, I think Riley Sampson has been stirring the pot when it comes to him. She does not like the fact your coffee shop is succeeding where hers failed. You can be sure I defended you whenever his name popped up. I'm glad hiring Joe temporarily worked out good."

"Yes, me too." Bridget set her fork down, suddenly quite full. Why it bothered her to hear Joe criticized, she couldn't say. It wasn't as if she didn't have the same thoughts herself about him at times. But he'd actually been monopolizing conversations with customers less often lately, and she'd noticed a sense of pride in him the past few weeks.

Mac asked Tess if she was still considering buying another horse, and, thankfully, the topic of Joe was abandoned.

When everyone was finished eating, Bridget helped clear the table, while Mac and Sawyer filled a sink with soapy water and began doing the dishes. Ken excused himself to rest.

Kaylee sidled up to her. "Guess what?"

"What?" Bridget couldn't help but smile at her chipper tone.

"Tanner and Fiona broke up."

"They did not." She used her most shocked voice.

"They did." Kaylee's excitement soared to next level. "He's been working on the junior's class float, and afterward, we all hang out for a while."

Bridget lifted her palm for a high five, which Kaylee slapped.

"I told you, he's been eyeing you." It was true. He came in every Monday and Wednesday when Kaylee worked. Always with a group of friends, and he made a point to say goodbye to her specifically.

"What are you two whispering about?" Mac asked over his shoulder.

"Nothing," Kaylee replied. With her hand covering her mouth, she giggled.

Tess charged into the kitchen with the final remnants of the meal. "Okay, I think we should wait at least an hour before pie. In the meantime, how about some games?"

"Games?" Bridget liked the sound of that. "Sure."

The color drained from Kaylee's face as she excused herself.

"Is something wrong with Kaylee?" Tess asked.

"I don't know." Bridget frowned as the girl disappeared down the hall to the bathroom.

"I mention games and you'd think I'd announced we were going to swim with sharks or jump from an airplane." Tess took plastic containers out of the cupboard to stash the remaining leftovers.

Bridget debated if she should check on Kaylee or give her some space. Mac must have noticed her absence, too, because he had his worried look on as he approached, toweling off his hands. "Where's Kay?"

"Bathroom."

"She all right?"

"I don't know." Maybe the girl needed a few minutes to work through whatever had set her off.

"What do you mean you don't know?" He scowled. "Did something happen?"

"I'm not sure."

His eyebrows furrowed as if he was mentally reviewing everything that could be wrong. Bridget could sense his mounting anxiety. Mac pivoted like he was going to check on her, but she put her hand on his arm, stopping him.

"Why don't you give her a minute?" Bridget said gently.

"I don't need you telling me what to do." He shook her hand off and stalked away.

A cold finger traced down her spine. He might as well have told her to *shut up, outsider*. Her good feelings vanished.

The real her kept sneaking out, kept assuming it was safe to be herself. It wasn't.

Mac didn't want the real her. No one did.

Mac rapped twice on the bathroom door. "You okay, Kaylee?"

"I'm fine." The sound of a flush, then water running, greeted him. He stood in the hall as fears circled like vultures in his mind. He'd been drying dishes with Sawyer when he heard the happy note in Kaylee's voice. Then he'd turned and watched her bright face fall, the joy draining from it in a flash.

Something had happened. And he was going to find out what it was one way or the other.

He crossed his arms over his chest. The door opened a crack. Slowly, Kaylee opened it and her eyes widened at him standing there.

"What happened?" He broadened his stance.

"Nothing." Her face was splotchy. Had she been crying?

"Something happened." He hated seeing her in pain.

She hugged her sweater tightly to her body. "Can we go home?"

"Yes." He was more than ready to leave. This entire meal had been way out of his comfort zone. Thanksgiving suppers were typically spent with Randy and Austin at their ranch. The three of them would order up a Thanksgiving meal from the grocery store, watch football and relax.

But Randy and Austin were spending it with Hannah's family this year, leaving him and Kaylee on their own. He wasn't used to china plates and homemade food and seeing Bridget's beautiful face across from him.

"I don't want to play games." Kaylee tugged on her sleeves, gripping the ends. "That's what Mom and I did on Thanksgiving. We'd watch the parade in the morning, have a big turkey dinner delivered, and when it was done, we'd play stuff like Yahtzee and Spoons."

Mac hadn't realized… "Did Dad play with you guys?" He couldn't imagine any scenario where his father would play Yahtzee. But maybe the three of them had been a real family.

A family he'd never been a part of.

"Dad? Yahtzee?" Her voice lilted and her color returned. "Yeah, right. He barely made it through a slice of pie before going to his office."

Why that comforted him he didn't care to think about.

Kaylee turned to stare down the hall. He winced. He'd been rude to Bridget. Really rude. For no reason.

"Come on. We'll take off." He felt for his keys in his pockets.

"Wait." She shook her head. "I need to talk to Bridget first."

He ran his tongue over his teeth as she scurried away. Always talking to Bridget. Confiding in Bridget. Never trusting him with anything.

Reluctantly, he returned to the dining room. Now that the table was clear and the dishes done, Tess and Sawyer were busy setting up a board game. Clue, from the looks of it. Kaylee and Bridget faced each other near the counter, talking in low tones he couldn't make out.

Bridget reached over and brushed some of Kaylee's hair behind her ear, giving her a tender look. Kaylee nodded at whatever she said and gave her a quick hug. Then they came over to the table.

"Oh, good, are you ready to play?" Tess smiled at them as they each took out a chair.

Wait? Why was Kaylee sitting? He thought they were getting out of here.

Then Tess glanced at him. "Mac? Are you in?"

"I don't know." He caught Kaylee's eyes and gave her the look that said, *Are you sure about this?* She nodded with a mixture of fear, longing and anticipation. He pulled out a chair. "I guess I'm in."

A minute ago, he'd been ready to take Kaylee home. Now, he was stuck playing Clue with the woman he'd been horrible to for no good reason. Happy Thanksgiving.

Everyone picked their playing pieces while Tess dealt the cards. Tucker sat on Sawyer's lap and hopped the green piece on the spaces in front of him. Mac sneaked a look at Bridget, but she didn't look his way. In fact, he got the impression she was avoiding his end of the table.

He didn't blame her.

The game started, and he kept an eye on Kaylee. Was this too hard—playing games without her mom? For the first fifteen minutes or so, she seemed subdued. But as the game wore on, everyone got louder, including her. Tess won the first round, and when Sawyer made a joke about her competitive side and hiding the candlesticks from her, she glared at him—and even Bridget chuckled.

Mac tried to ignore the guilt mounting inside him. Yes, he'd been rude to Bridget, and, no, she hadn't deserved it. But…

He owed her an apology.

Plain and simple.

It would have to wait until they were alone, though, and from the looks of it, that would be a while.

The next two hours were filled with laughter, a lot of pumpkin pie and coffee. Bridget insisted on brewing it, and whatever she added made it taste better than he imagined possible. They played more games. By the time they finished, Tucker's yawns grew bigger.

"We'd better be taking off." Mac helped clear the last of the dessert plates. Kaylee was right behind him with the remaining coffee cups. He still hadn't had the chance to apologize to Bridget.

"Want us to give you a ride home?" Kaylee asked her.

His stomach clenched. *No. Please say no.*

"Umm…" Bridget glanced at Sawyer, then at Mac, then back to Kaylee. A fly caught in a spiderweb couldn't have looked more stuck.

"Would you mind?" Sawyer asked Mac. "I've got to run out and check on a pregnant cow. The old girl worried me this morning, and I won't feel right waiting until tomorrow."

"Sure. No problem."

After they all exchanged hugs and raved about the meal, Mac, Kaylee and Bridget headed outside. Should he apologize now? Or wait until he dropped her off?

"Can I drive?" Bridget kept her head high as she marched in clipped strides. "I need to get used to driving in the dark."

"It's Thanksgiving." He didn't know why he said it.

"I'm aware."

Kaylee was already well ahead of them. He held out the keys to Bridget. She halted.

"Hey, I'm sorry," he said. "About earlier. I was rude."

She nodded, staring at the ground momentarily before meeting his gaze. "It's okay. You were right. You don't need me telling you what to do."

Then she took the keys from his hand and strode to the truck, leaving him staring after her, wondering why he was careful about everyone's feelings except Bridget's. He never would have said those things to one of the guys or to Kaylee.

Why was he being so awful to the woman he thought so highly of? The one he couldn't stop thinking about?

He wasn't solving that mystery tonight. Something told him he'd be better off not solving it ever.

Chapter Eight

"We did it!" Bridget high-fived Kaylee as they left their final driver's ed class on Saturday. She let out a satisfied sigh. She'd passed the exam and had her waiver for the skills test. All she had to do now was go to the DMV and get her license.

She didn't feel ready yet, though.

"We finished. Can you believe it?" Kaylee beamed with happiness. "I actually was less nervous driving with the instructor this week. I might even ask Mac if I can drive home today."

"You should." Snow was falling in big flakes. The prettiest kind. Bridget pulled a stocking cap out of her coat pocket and tugged it over her head. Mac's truck was nowhere to be seen, which was odd. He'd never been late to pick them up.

Had something happened? An accident? No, he'd probably had to check on one of the calves. And why did she care? It had been two days since Thanksgiving. While she'd appreciated his apology, it didn't change the fact he thought she should mind her own business.

"Where's Mac?" Kaylee said while typing on her phone.

"I don't know. I'm sure he'll be here soon." Holding up

her certificate, Bridget snapped a quick picture of it and texted it to Sawyer. Shivering, she mentally reviewed the plan for the day.

First up, relieve Joe of his duties and give him the thank-you gift she'd made him—a basket with assorted coffee beans, an *Employee of the Month* mug and homemade snickerdoodles.

Next, she had to decorate her apartment for Christmas. She and Joe had gussied up the shop with white string lights. Deep red ornaments contrasted with the greenery they'd tucked throughout the space. Brewed Awakening couldn't look more festive, but her apartment? Zero Christmas cheer.

"A bunch of us are going out to Bryce Colder's ranch later." Kaylee slipped her phone into her pocket.

"That sounds fun. What are you going to do there?"

"Have a bonfire and pizza. Tanner's going."

"Oh? Are you nervous?"

"A little bit." Her hazel eyes shimmered. "I'm not sure what to expect. And I don't know what to wear."

"Hmm…bonfire? Something warm. Jeans, for sure. A sweater. Bring gloves and a hat."

"I don't have a cute one like yours."

Bridget took off her stocking cap and handed it to her with a wink. "Now you do."

"I can't take your hat." Her eyes grew round.

"Borrow it for tonight. You can bring it back next week."

"Are you sure?"

"Of course, I'm sure." Bridget pointed to the parking lot entrance, relieved to see Mac's truck. "Oh, look, there's your brother."

"I haven't told him about tonight. Do you think he'll let me go?"

"Do you think he won't?" Bridget asked gently.

"He will. I just feel… I don't know…funny asking."

"Because of Tanner." Bridget hooked her arm in Kaylee's and headed to the truck.

"I guess."

"You two aren't dating or girlfriend and boyfriend, right?"

"No!" She shook her head and her brown hair swished behind her neck. "I have a hard time saying more than three words to him."

"I find it really hard to talk to cute guys, too."

"You do?" Kaylee glanced up at her.

"Yeah, I do." Bridget looked at Mac, sitting in the driver's seat. Through the windshield she could see he was on the phone and looked annoyed. "Don't worry. I have a feeling Tanner will seek you out. You won't have to do a thing."

"I hope so." Kaylee exhaled dramatically before opening the door to the back seat.

Bridget climbed into the passenger seat. Usually, she drove them back to the coffee shop, but Mac showed no signs of moving from the driver's seat as he continued his phone call.

"I hear you, Dina… I know…yes, you're right. Listen, I've got to go. Yes, I'll think about it." He hung up, tossing the phone onto the center console before rubbing his hand down his cheek to his chin.

Bridget wanted to ask him if everything was okay, but he'd probably tell her it was none of her concern, so she buckled up and stayed silent.

"Last class, huh?" Mac made a concerted effort to be pleasant.

She was surprised at the sudden mood change. How much of Mac's patience was practiced? And how much did it cost him?

"Yes, and I passed!" Kaylee thrust her papers up to him. "I can get my license!"

"This is great! I'm proud of you." He grinned back at her. "But you need a lot more practice first."

Bridget wanted to wave her papers in his face and yell, "Me, too! Me, too!" and hear how proud he was of her. How pathetic was that? Wanting praise for something most people had been doing their entire adult lives?

Her phone chimed. Sawyer texted her.

Congratulations! We need to get you a car.

Her chest swelled at his thoughtfulness.

"Did you want to drive?" Mac glanced at Bridget.

"Uh, that's okay."

He regarded her a few moments. "Is that your certificate?" He pointed to the paper in her lap.

"Yeah." Bridget nodded.

With two fingers, he beckoned her to hand it to him. When she did, he read it and gave her a soft smile. "It took a lot of guts to get this."

"Thanks." Shyness crept in.

"Hand your phone over and hold it up." He handed her the certificate as she gave him her phone. "Say cheese."

Cheese? She blinked as he snapped the photo.

Kaylee's head popped up between the seats. "Her eyes were closed. Take another."

Bridget willed herself to look like a normal human being as he took a few more pictures. Then Mac handed her the phone, cranked the radio and backed out of the spot. The fact he'd acknowledged it wasn't easy for her to do this filled in an empty spot in her heart even Sawyer couldn't fill.

Mac understood. She wasn't sure how, but he did.

Kaylee's voice carried from the back seat as she sang "It's Beginning to Look a Lot Like Christmas" with Michael Bublé. Her voice was high and clear. She didn't miss a note.

Bridget turned back to her. "I didn't know you could sing like that."

"I didn't either," Mac said.

She blushed and shrugged. "Mom and I sang a lot. She was in charge of the Christmas choir, so we practiced all the songs together every year."

"You must miss her. What a special memory." Bridget swiped through the photos Mac had taken and inwardly laughed at the one with her eyes closed. It might be her favorite.

"Yeah." Kaylee sounded wistful.

"Our church has a choir, Kay, if you're interested." Mac pulled onto Main Street.

Crickets from the back seat. That suggestion wasn't going over well.

Bridget noted how pretty all the storefronts looked with their wreaths and Christmas lights as the snow danced down. Then Mac parked, and as she got out, her purse tipped over onto the floor mat. She grabbed her lip gloss, keys and pen before they could roll onto the pavement. Stuffing them back in the purse, she did a quick search for anything else that might have fallen. She didn't see anything.

"Thanks again." Bridget waved to Mac, then turned to Kaylee. "Have fun tonight."

Kaylee bit her lower lip as her eyes sparkled.

"Hey, Bridget," Mac called.

She turned back.

"Congratulations, again. On finishing the classes." His cheeks grew red.

"Thanks. I couldn't have done it without you." Bridget went to the entrance, only looking back when she heard the truck pulling away. A part of her wanted to invite them both over to help decorate her apartment tonight. But Kaylee had plans, and Mac was Mac, so…

She hauled the door open, inhaled the magnificent aroma of coffee and smiled at the sight of an almost full house.

She was blessed. Her dream of spending her days living the rural life in Sunrise Bend had taken a giant leap forward today. And she had Mac to thank, regardless of how he felt about her.

He was drawn to Bridget like cows to barley. Later that evening, Mac stood in front of the door to the stairway leading to her apartment. He'd just dropped off Kaylee at Bryce's—Mac still wasn't certain it had been wise to let her go—and instead of driving straight home and enjoying a rare night alone like in the good old days, he'd driven here.

A half-moon illuminated the black sky, and big clouds played peekaboo with the stars. The door mocked him. Should he go up? Or turn around and leave?

It wasn't like he needed reassurance about Kaylee or anything. If he mentioned his concern about this teenage gathering, Bridget would probably tell him he'd been wrong to let her go or, on the flip side, that Kaylee would be fine.

Something else had drawn him here, and it wasn't the tiny tube of lotion he'd found in his truck. The small container of hand cream in his palm was the weakest excuse he'd ever used to visit a woman. As soon as he'd seen it wedged under the floor mat, he'd known he was coming here tonight.

There was a realness—an openness—to his relationship with Bridget he had never experienced before.

He flung the door open and took the steps two at a time. At the landing, he paused in front of her apartment door, trying to figure out what to say. Music played from inside.

What if she had someone over? That would be embarrassing.

Holding his breath, he listened for voices. Nothing.

Just give her the hand cream. See what happens.

He knocked. The door opened an inch or two, but a chain lock prevented it from opening more. One eye peeked out, widened, then the door shut and the sound of the chain sliding made him straighten.

Her big smile drove every other thought away. He'd memorized how white her teeth were and how her straight nose set off her cheekbones, but being up close to her still managed to knock him out.

"What are you doing here?" She ushered him inside.

"Found this on the floor." He held the tube between his index finger and thumb. Then he tossed it to her. "Thought you might need it."

Her nose scrunched in delight as she caught it. "Thanks. I can't live without this stuff. 'Tis the season for chapped hands."

Mac chuckled and stood there in his unzipped coat, taking in the place. All the decorations they'd purchased a few weeks ago were spilling out of bags and boxes on the floor just outside the kitchen. Something smelled like pumpkin and chocolate all rolled into one. The music he'd heard was an upbeat Christmas song, and every light in the apartment seemed to be on.

"Want to help me decorate?" she asked. "Or are you in a hurry?"

"I'm not in a hurry."

He shrugged off his coat and hung it on a hook next to the door.

"What smells so good?" he asked, following her into the kitchen where cookies and cupcakes lined the counters.

"I'm on a baking spree. It's too hard to make everything each night, so I'm trying to bake twice a week and freeze some of it. I thaw the ones I'm selling the night before. So far, so good."

"Mind if I try one?" He pointed to a muffin, dark orange in color.

"Go for it. That's pumpkin chocolate chip."

He peeled the wrapper from it and took a bite. His taste buds exploded as he sank into the softness of the muffin. It tasted like…home, autumn, domestic bliss.

He didn't have much experience with the last one. But Bridget made him feel like he was this close.

"I'm kind of liking this whole baking thing." Bridget cracked open the oven to check on whatever was in there. "Never thought I'd be doing this on weekends. But, then, I never thought I'd be living in Wyoming with my own coffee shop, either. Funny how life works out, huh?"

"Yeah, it is." He finished off the muffin in two more bites and was tempted to snatch another. Instead, he crossed over to the table and pulled out a chair, sitting on it backward to face her. A feeling of peace washed over him.

Here in this cheerful, messy kitchen, he didn't have to worry about a thing. In fact, none of his problems—the donation requests, the limping calf he'd found yesterday, his concerns about Kaylee—had air to breathe in here. He could set them aside for a little while.

"So, I'm assuming you let Kaylee go to Bryce's." Bridget slipped off the oven mitts, set them next to the stove and leaned against the counter, watching him.

"I did." A spurt of jealousy popped up that Bridget already knew about the party. "Just dropped her off."

Smiling, she nodded. He waited for her to ask questions about it or give advice. But she didn't. A bag full of white plastic snowflakes coated in clear glitter near his feet drew his attention. He lifted one up. "Where are you putting these?"

"I'm not sure." She bit the corner of her bottom lip. "This is kind of new for me."

"Decorating for Christmas?"

"That, too. I'm not used to having so much space." She looked around the room, shaking her head in wonder. "I usually set a teeny tree on an end table. My apartment was a studio. So, to have a big kitchen and a big living room, and my own laundry and two whole bedrooms? It's amazing."

Mac averted his gaze, ashamed at all he took for granted. In his mind, this apartment was small, old and outdated. Yet, Bridget acted like it was a luxury condo.

She tapped her chin. "I have no idea how to start decorating."

"Well, the stylist Dad sends every year takes care of all that…" He frowned. The stylist Dad *used* to send every year… Mac had called the company, based in Jackson, Wyoming, in September, and they'd decked his halls last weekend. Hadn't come cheap, but he couldn't imagine decorating the massive home on his own.

Kaylee had liked how it turned out, but she'd insisted on unpacking special ornaments to hang on the tree, too. He'd helped her, and they'd talked about how they wanted to celebrate this year. Both had agreed to keep it low-key.

"A stylist, huh?" She grinned, wagging her eyebrows. "Fancy."

He started to protest, but the oven timer went off, and she bent over to take out the trays. Cookies this time.

"What you're really saying is you're no help in the decorating department, right?" she teased.

"Put like that…" He rubbed the back of his neck. "I'm willing to learn, if that counts for anything."

"It counts for everything." She deftly slid a spatula under a cookie and moved it to a cooling rack. Then she repeated the motion until all the cookies had been transferred. She turned the oven off, untied her apron—the same one she wore to the coffee shop every day—and closed the distance between them.

His heart hammered as she approached. His body stilled. What was she doing? Why was she getting so close? He had half a mind to draw her to him, to kiss her…

"Let me grab these lights, and we can get started." She reached past his shoulder for another plastic bag.

As she walked away, he let out the breath he hadn't realized he'd been holding. What had gotten into him?

He stood a little too quickly, tipping the chair. He righted it. Then he joined Bridget in the living room.

"I don't know how to put the tree together." She waved to the box still sitting where he'd left it a few weeks ago.

He scratched his chin. "Let's open it up and see what's in there. Shouldn't be too hard."

"Okay."

Mac dragged the box to the center of the room, pulled out his pocketknife and sliced the box open. Then he took out the sections of the artificial tree, ignoring the booklet on top.

"I think these are the directions." Bridget snatched up the booklet.

"We don't need them."

She rolled her eyes and opened to the first page while he continued to empty the box.

"It says to put the stand together."

"Stand? What stand?" He dug through the tree sections and found two thin, oblong curved metal pipes. He held them up. "These?"

"I think so." Tracing her finger down the page, she sighed. "Are there screws anywhere?"

A quick search yielded a small plastic bag with screws.

"Oh, good. Put the stand together like this—" she came over, getting on her knees beside him, and showed him the diagram "—and screw it tight so it forms an X."

He could smell the medley of chocolate and coffee and vanilla and cinnamon on her, and it made him want to lean in and…

"Mac?"

He looked at her, only inches from him, and held her gaze. Her brown eyes gleamed, and his gaze dropped to her lips. He couldn't look away. What would they taste like?

She thrust the booklet in his hand, shaking him out of whatever state he was in. "An X."

Fine. She wasn't into him like that. Point taken.

He glanced at her again, and all it took was one peek from her and he knew—she *was* into him like that. She either didn't want to admit it or wasn't ready to take the next step.

Neither was he.

Clearing his throat, he turned his attention to the diagram. Directions? What self-respecting guy read the directions? He set them on the floor next to him and proceeded to put the stand together.

"There. It's an X." He set it on the hardwood floor next to him.

"You did it!" She beamed. He was surprised she didn't start clapping. And he wouldn't mind if she did. It was nice being appreciated for once.

"Now that we got the stand done," she said, "how do these branches fit together?"

Fifteen minutes later, the tree was standing.

"I need a break before we fluff the rest of the branches." Bridget collapsed onto the couch, and Mac sat on the other end of it. "So, tell me about how you do Christmas. Did you spend the holidays with your dad, stepmom and Kaylee?"

A sinking sensation overcame him. "No. I stayed on the ranch. Had to be there for the cattle."

"Surely you could have taken a few days off?"

"If I had thought my dad would be there for two days, I probably would have. The fathers you see in the Christmas movies? He wasn't that kind of man."

"Oh, I'm sorry."

"What about you? Good memories of Christmases with your dad before he died?" He shifted to watch her and was struck by how sad she seemed.

"He wasn't that kind of father, either." The sadness dissipated. "If you didn't spend Christmas with your family, how did you spend it?"

The few times they'd scratched the surface on their pasts, Mac noticed Bridget changed the subject quickly. She clearly had bad memories, and he could relate.

"Well, the first thing I do is make a big thermos of coffee, eat at least two cinnamon rolls Mary Lutz bakes for me, then I sit in front of the Christmas tree and I pray. Hope that doesn't sound weird."

She shook her head, her eyes shining brightly.

"I'm just real thankful God never gives up on me." Mac let his knees splay. "Christmas makes me think about spiritual things more."

"Me, too," she said.

"I saddle up one of the horses—usually Caesar—and

ride out to feed and check cattle. I love it when it snows on Christmas. I don't love it when it's all muddy."

"I can see that." She brought one knee up, hugging it as she faced him. "What else?"

"Later, I usually share a meal with Austin and Randy, although this year will be different now that Randy's moved out and Austin has the baby. They're spending Christmas with Hannah's family."

"Bummer." She nodded. "Things change. There goes your tradition. I suppose it would have changed anyhow with Kaylee here."

"Yeah." He knew his traditions needed to be replaced with something Kaylee-friendly. It was why they'd gone to Sawyer's for Thanksgiving. That way she could enjoy a holiday with people she'd grown comfortable with.

Frankly, he'd enjoyed the holiday with them, too. Except for the part when he'd hurt Bridget's feelings.

"What will you do this year?" she asked.

"I don't know." He didn't like the thought of not having his big thermos of coffee and two cinnamon rolls and the prayers in front of the tree.

"Well, you should still have the coffee and cinnamon rolls and prayer time. They're part of your tradition. Kaylee won't mind."

Until this moment, he'd felt like he had to change everything to accommodate his sister—hearing Bridget say he should keep the parts he liked made his heart flex with gratitude.

This was why he liked being around Bridget.

She got him.

The good feeling deflated. She got the parts he was willing to share, not the entire him. He'd never tell her that his father viewed him as an easily manipulated wimp.

Mac couldn't pursue these feelings he had for her. He

couldn't take the chance of someone else having control over everything he loved. Like the ranch and Kaylee. They were too important to screw up.

The bell clanged in Brewed Awakening late Monday afternoon, and Bridget looked up from where she was steaming milk to see Kaylee rush in. After putting the final touches on the cappuccino, Bridget wiped her hands down her apron.

"You look happy," Bridget said. She half expected Kaylee to declare that she and Tanner were dating. Yesterday, the girl had texted her that she'd had a fun time at the bonfire, but she hadn't gone into much detail.

"Guess what? I'm joining the church's Christmas choir!" Kaylee's hazel eyes glowed gold.

Those were the last words Bridget ever expected to come out of her mouth. "You are?"

"Yeah." She nodded. "Let me put this in the back and I'll tell you all about it."

The bell clanged again, and Bridget's good cheer shriveled as Janet Jones and another woman came inside. Janet had been back twice and had lectured Bridget on how Joe working there would drive away her business. Bridget had just politely wished her a good day after giving the woman her macchiatos.

Something about Janet grated on her nerves.

Kaylee rushed back, tying her apron, then she skidded to a halt next to the cash register when she saw the two women.

"Hi, Mrs. Jones," Kaylee said with a pleasant smile. "What can I get for you?"

"Kaylee, look at you!" Janet exclaimed, beaming. Kaylee gave Bridget a questioning glance. Bridget merely shrugged. "It's wonderful to see you working so hard. Enterprising girl. Please tell your brother to call Dina. She's been trying to get a hold of him."

"I'll tell him, Mrs. Jones."

Janet proceeded to place her order. As Kaylee cashed the ladies out, Janet turned to her companion. "What did I tell you? Night and day without Joe here."

A bitter feeling crawled across Bridget's chest. Who did this lady think she was? Complaining about sweet Joe?

Don't say anything, Bridget. It's not worth it.

"What do you mean?" Kaylee asked, her features twisting in confusion.

Janet faced her. "Joe Schlock never knows when to stop talking. It makes people uncomfortable. He's bad for business."

Bridget held her breath, silently urging Kaylee not to respond. She couldn't afford to alienate customers in this small of a town.

"Mr. Schlock is so nice." Kaylee frowned. "He's good for business."

Janet patted Kaylee's hand. "You'll understand when you're older."

Kaylee snatched her hand away. "I understand now." Her tone had an edge to it.

"I see." Janet straightened, pursing her lips and flicking a knowing glance at her friend.

"Why don't you make our orders to go."

Bridget poured their coffee drinks into take-out cups. The ladies took the cups and marched out the door. Would they ever come back?

Were they going to spread bad news about her shop?

She needed every sale. Sure, she was making enough to pay her expenses and for Kaylee's and Joe's wages, but she'd had a lot of one-time purchases to make lately. She'd used most of her savings to move out here and furnish the coffee shop. And she still needed to buy a car…

"I don't like her." Kaylee glared at the door long after they'd left. "She's fake."

"She's just set in her ways."

"Yeah, well, she's all nicey-nice to me because I'm Mac's sister—and everyone around here knows we're rich—but Mr. Schlock is the nicest guy on the planet and she acts like he's dirt."

"Joe does like to talk."

Kaylee faced her then, her anger flaring. "I thought *you* at least would stick up for him."

If Bridget had been slapped in the face, she wouldn't feel worse.

Kaylee was right. She *should* have stuck up for him.

Shame poured over her in waves as she moved to the other end of the counter to restock coffee stirrers and sugar packets. In all her years, she couldn't remember a time she liked herself less.

When had she become so fearful about what other people said about her? Thought about her?

A fifteen-year-old had more courage and fire than she did. Without Joe, Bridget never would have been able to keep the shop open on Saturdays.

He hadn't scared customers away. She had the receipts to prove it.

Bending down for the box of stirrers, she tried to catch her breath. *Is this who I want to be? Hiding the real me for the rest of my life? Too afraid of losing customers to stick up for my friends?*

She placed her hand on the shelf to steady herself. *God, I want to be bold, like Kaylee. Help me overcome this fear.*

If Bridget didn't make some changes soon, she might

not recognize who she was. But what if she spoke up, and everyone in this town turned on her?

She couldn't lose this. Not the coffee shop, not the apartment, not the town.

Not when she was starting to feel like she belonged here.

But did she really belong here if she wasn't letting anyone see the real her?

Chapter Nine

Should he ask Bridget if she wanted to practice driving with him or not? Mac sat at the counter in Brewed Awakening Wednesday evening. Kaylee was in the back room getting her stuff. Bridget was nowhere to be seen.

As far as he knew, Bridget hadn't gotten her license yet. More practice wouldn't hurt her. Even if she had gotten it.

Clearly, he was looking for an excuse to spend time with her.

Bridget appeared in the doorway leading to the back room. With an easy smile, she strolled behind the counter to where he sat, cocked her head to the side and pointed to where his fingertips were tapping the counter.

"Want a coffee for the road?"

He flattened his fingers on the counter, not taking his gaze off her. "Will it keep me up half the night?"

"It might."

"Then, yeah, why not. Time to live dangerously."

"Coffee at five thirty is living dangerously?" She laughed as she pivoted and took hold of the coffee pot, then filled a take-out cup. She slid it over to him and placed a lid next to it.

"To me it is." He ignored the coffee and instead, drank

her in. Half of her dark brown hair was pulled back into a high bun, and the other half fell over her shoulders. She wore her typical work outfit. The sparrow necklace drew his attention. He was sure there was a story behind it.

"Have you gotten your license yet?"

"Not yet."

"Want to get more practice in?"

"Actually, yes, I do. I know I've got the basic skills down, but I'd feel better if I could get behind the wheel a few more times."

Just what he'd been hoping. "Well, Kaylee and I are grabbing a bite to eat before I drop her off at the church for choir practice. Why don't I swing by after?"

"I have a better idea," Kaylee said coming up to him. She let her backpack rest near her feet as she zipped her coat. "Why don't you come to the restaurant with us, Bridget? Then you guys can drive while I'm at choir."

"Oh, um." Bridget stared at the counter for a moment. Then she looked at Kaylee, then him, her nose crinkling. "I'd better not. I should—"

"You need to eat supper." Kaylee hiked the backpack onto her shoulder.

Mac held his breath. He wanted her to join them. He wanted it a little too much.

"Okay. Let me throw my apron in the back and finish closing up." She hurried to the back room.

He stood, the steaming coffee in hand. "How did school go?"

"Meh." She dragged her toe along the ground. "I wanted to call you so bad to pick me up during Lit class. My head was throbbing."

He stiffened. Ever since she'd started working here, Kaylee hadn't missed any school.

"Did something happen?"

"No, not really. I don't like the book we're reading. And when Mrs. Deacon drones on and on, my mind starts wandering, and my stupid head drifts back to this summer. You know, to before the plane crash."

He shouldn't be surprised or relieved, but he was both. Surprised she was bringing up the crash; relieved her headaches weren't due to something more. Something he'd know if he wasn't so lousy at this parenting thing.

"We don't have to talk about it if it upsets you."

Her cheeks grew splotchy. "It does upset me. All I can think about is how I wish I could hug Mom one more time. I wish I could tell her about all the things that are happening. I wish she and I were doing the choir again tonight—together."

He set the cup on the counter and wrapped his arms around her, resting his chin on the top of her head.

"I'm sorry, Kay. I wish all of that for you, too." He held her for a minute before she backed away. He bent to look in her eyes. "Next time, call me and I'll come pick you up."

"I can't skip school. I'll lose my job." Her throat worked. "I went to the nurse and got a Tylenol like you told me to."

"Hey, you don't have to keep it together all the time. If you're not feeling well or you're upset, I'll pick you up. Don't ever think I won't."

"I know." She nodded. Then she looked away. "The parade is this weekend. Our float is pretty chill."

He debated saying something more. He wanted her to know that this coffee shop job wasn't the be-all and end-all. She could miss school now and then without worrying about losing her position. Was she putting too much pressure on herself?

"Thanks for waiting." Bridget strolled over, wearing her winter coat and pulling on her gloves. "Ready?"

* * *

Well, this was a nice change. Bridget held up the laminated menu at Bubba's, the barbecue joint on the outskirts of town, and reviewed her options. Burger and fries? Grilled chicken breast? Or pulled pork? They all sounded amazing. And best of all, she wouldn't be eating alone.

As the muffled conversations carried on around them, she glanced at Kaylee, to her left, and to Mac, sitting across from them. He was dunking his straw into a large soda, and Kaylee was pretending not to be interested in a table near the corner. Tanner was there with a few other boys and girls Bridget recognized. They waved and called Kaylee over.

"What do they want?" Mac flicked his thumb their way.

"I don't know." Kaylee's voice was high.

"Why don't you go find out?"

"Really?"

"Yeah. They obviously want to talk to you."

"Okay." She slid out of the booth and picked her way over to them.

Mac met Bridget's eyes. "What's that all about?"

If he didn't know, she wasn't going to be the one to fill him in. She smiled and shrugged. Kaylee rushed back.

"Is it okay if I eat with them? I don't have to, but they asked, and…" She twisted her hands together.

"Go ahead. Eat with your friends. Bring me the bill when you're done." He waved her off, and she beamed before working her way back to the table.

After a waiter took their orders, Bridget took a moment to get a better look at the place. Booths lined the walls. Wooden tables took up the rest of the room. A country song played through the speakers, and a large television was mounted near the bar. Best of all, it smelled delicious, like comfort food.

"Are you ready for the open house this weekend?" Mac asked. "The parade kicks off at ten. Kaylee's going to Lydia's Friday night, and they're getting to the parade early so they can hand out candy next to the float. I told her I'd be there watching for her."

"I'm ready." Yesterday, she'd asked Joe if he'd help her out on Saturday since she assumed it would be really busy. He'd assured her he would and had even given her ideas for a few new coffee drinks. He'd also warned her that Riley was setting up a coffee and hot chocolate stand on one of the corners.

Competition. She'd make the best of it.

"Mac, just the man I wanted to see." A burly man wearing a pair of jeans, a basic white shirt, a large buckle on his belt and a navy sports jacket clapped Mac on the shoulder. "Have you had a chance to think about the pavilion?"

"Hi, Glen. No, I haven't. Been pretty busy." Mac's face, usually open, closed like the shades she pulled over her front window every night.

"I understand. The cattle take up a lot of time." He rocked back on his heels. "Well, listen, I got a quote and…"

The man droned on for several minutes, but after the first few sentences, Bridget tuned out. Why was he expecting Mac to pay for a pavilion for a private fishing organization? Shouldn't they pay for it themselves? And why did he think it was okay to interrupt their supper like this?

"I'll think about it."

Bridget looked up at Mac's curt tone. It was one she hadn't heard before. Well, that wasn't quite true. She'd caught a hint of it when he'd been speaking on the phone with the woman wanting money for the booster club—Janet's daughter-in-law, if she remembered correctly.

"Great, great. That's all I ask." Glen seemed to realize Mac wasn't alone and turned to Bridget. "Well, if it isn't our new coffee gal. I'm Glen Slate." He slid a card out of his wallet and handed it to her. "You need insurance? Call me. I'll set you up."

"Thank you. I'm taken care of." She glanced at his card, then slipped it into her purse. She was all set on business insurance, and she'd had to buy auto insurance before taking the driver's ed class. Another reason she needed to get her license soon. Why pay for insurance if she wasn't using it?

"No problem." He held his palms out near his chest and backed up a step. "If something changes…"

The waiter arrived with their food, and the man left.

"Does that happen often?" She squirted a blob of ketchup next to her fries, then took the top bun off her burger and swirled ketchup on it, too.

"What?" He shook pepper on his baked potato.

"People randomly asking you for money?"

"They're not…well…yeah." He tilted his head as if to say *go figure*.

"Why?" She dipped a fry in the ketchup and took a bite. Crispy and delicious.

"There are a lot of good causes and not enough money to fund them all." His diplomatic tone didn't fool her. He didn't like it, either.

"Why do they ask you?"

"Because I have money."

"Yeah, so?" She picked up the burger in both hands and bit into it. *Mmm, yeah, that was good.*

He finished chewing a bite of his pulled pork sandwich and regarded her thoughtfully. "What do you mean?"

"Nothing. Just thinking." Just thinking she wouldn't like people expecting her to fund all their pet projects even if she did have money, which she didn't. Maybe that made her stingy. "Does it bother you?"

"No." His jaw tightened. He met her gaze. "Yes."

"It would bother me, too." The more she thought about it, the more it irritated her that Mac had to deal with this on an ongoing basis. "Are you going to give him the money?"

He grew very interested in his plate of food.

"I'm sorry, I shouldn't have asked. It's none of my business." Regret soured her stomach. She didn't like when people nosed into her private affairs. She wished she could take the words back.

"No, it's all right." His gray eyes were clear again. "Honestly, I don't know. I've been putting off the requests for a long time. I don't want to deal with them."

"I wouldn't want to, either." She continued eating her burger.

"If you were me, what would you do?"

Bridget almost choked on her bite. If she were him? Respected, well-liked, wealthy…kind?

"I guess it would depend."

"On what?" He wiped his mouth with his napkin and gave her his full attention.

"On where my heart was at." Why was he so attractive? Why did she feel like the restaurant disappeared when he looked at her like that? "What's a cause close to your heart?"

He sipped his drink while he reflected. Bridget kept munching on her fries.

"I haven't really thought about it, but I'd have to say cancer. Losing my mom so young was something I don't wish on anyone."

Her heart squeezed for him. And it brought to mind Ken and Tess and what Sawyer had told her about treatments being so far away.

"I feel bad for Tess having to drive Ken over an hour away for all his treatments."

"Huh." His eyebrows furrowed. "I'm surprised the family practice in town doesn't accommodate him. It's not as if Ken's the first resident of Sunrise Bend to get cancer."

"From what I hear at the coffee shop, the family practice is busy enough as it is, and they don't have the equipment or the personnel for his treatments."

"I suppose you're right." He opened his mouth to say something, then shut it just as quickly.

"What?" she asked.

"Nothing." He shook his head. "I was just thinking… I still have a lot of people pinning their hopes on me. I need to take care of it all soon."

Take care of it all? "The requests?"

"Yes. I've got decisions to make. And I'll be honest, I dread making them. Sometimes I wish it was like it was before my dad died. But then I remember how my hands were tied at the ranch, and I don't want that. I must sound pretty pathetic, huh? Complaining about my life."

"I don't think so. Why would you say that?"

"Poor rich guy." He let out a snort. "I have so much more than most people."

A sprout of shame burst through her. She'd thought as much several times in the past. But it wasn't true. His wealth didn't define him.

"You're so much more than your money, Mac." Heat rushed up her neck. She wasn't used to being this honest with anyone.

He caught her eye. "Thanks. I needed to hear that."

Kaylee returned and handed Mac her bill. She was positively glowing.

"Have fun?" Bridget asked.

She nodded, smiling brightly.

"Are you ready for choir practice?" Bridget asked as Kaylee slid into the booth next to her. "Nervous at all?"

"Yeah. I haven't sung since last year, and I'm not used to singing without Mom."

"It might be hard at first."

Mac looked up then. "If it's too hard, call me. I'll come get you."

Bridget refrained from glaring at him. She wouldn't ruin the moment. But didn't he realize he wasn't helping his sister by constantly giving her a way out of uncomfortable situations? The girl needed to work things out for herself instead of cutting and running at the first hint of conflict.

Kaylee could handle choir. Even if Mac was afraid she'd fall apart.

"Thanks for the tour, man," Blaine said.

Mac strode next to him. It was Friday morning, and he'd just shown Blaine his newly improved storage system for the winter feed. They'd moved outside where the sun broke through the thick clouds every now and then.

"How's it going now that you're running your own operation?" Mac stopped in front of the main horse paddock, where the majority of his horses were grazing. "Have you figured out what you want to name your half of the ranch?"

"South Mayer Canyon Ranch," Blaine said. "Jet's changing his to North Mayer Canyon Ranch."

"Keeping it in the family, I see."

"That's right." Blaine hooked his cowboy boot on the bottom rail of the fence. "Life sure changed in a year, huh?"

Mac leaned his forearm on the top of the fence and kept one eye on the horses, who were snorting happily in the chilly air, and the other on Blaine, who looked like he had something on his mind besides the winter feed storage. "You can say that again."

"Life sure changed in a year." Blaine grinned.

Mac laughed. Goofball.

"Seriously, though," Blaine said. "I feel out of sorts. Jet's always with Holly, planning their wedding. Erica's married and living far away, and Reagan's constantly making candles. On top of that Randy's engaged, and Austin has a kid. What in the world happened? A year ago, it's the six of us hanging out watching football, single as can be, and now everyone's paired off. What is going on?"

Mac was taken aback. Blaine was nothing if not eventempered. Where had all that come from?

Blaine shook his head. "I mean, I'm happy for them and all, but we haven't had a guys' night in months. It's couples and babies and toddlers and females. I miss Monday Night Football with you guys."

He hadn't thought about it much—probably because he hadn't had time to think with Kaylee's schedule keeping him so busy—but Blaine was right. He missed their guy time, too.

"Let's plan on getting together Monday," Mac said.

"Really?"

They discussed their favorite teams, the injured players, the coach that was recently fired and who they wanted to win in next week's matchups. This was one of the things Mac liked about Blaine—their friendship wasn't complicated. Football and ranching were enough for them both.

"Mom told me Kaylee joined the Christmas choir at church." Blaine shoved off from the fence. "Said she's a really good singer. How did you talk her into that?"

"Believe it or not, it was Kaylee's idea."

"I thought she was shy. Is she still missing school?"

"It's not so much shy as reserved with people she doesn't know well. And, no, ever since she started working at Brewed Awakening, she hasn't missed a day."

"That's good." They walked past the stables. "Jacob—

my new ranch hand—told me his little brother seems to like her."

"Who is it?" Mac stilled.

"Tanner Voss. You know, the one on the rodeo team?"

Mac pictured him instantly. He was a good-looking kid. He'd been in the town's paper several times for bull riding and barrel racing. Now that he was thinking about it, hadn't Tanner been one of the kids at the restaurant the other night? "He's too old for her."

"How old is she?" Blaine scratched his scruff.

"Fifteen."

"Well, I'm pretty sure Tanner's a junior, so I don't think he's robbing the cradle or anything."

"She's too young to be dating."

"No one said anything about dating."

"Good. She's got more sense than to go for a rodeo hound, anyway. She would have told me."

Blaine guffawed. "You think she's going to tell you when she's got a boyfriend?" The look he sent his way oozed skepticism.

"Why wouldn't she?" Mac glared. "We're close."

"You're dreaming. If she's going to tell anyone it's her best friend. I know how girls her age work. I have two sisters." Blaine's boots crunched on the gravel as they reached the stables.

Best friend. Lydia would know. Bridget would likely know, too.

"You look mad. I'm sorry. I thought you knew."

"Knew what? That some kid on the rodeo team has a thing for Kaylee? They aren't a couple or anything. There's nothing to know."

"Okay. Whatever you say." Blaine slid open the door to the stables. "Hey, did Dina Jones ever get a hold of you?"

"Only about a million times. Why?" He strode inside,

his eyes adjusting to the dim light. The rows of stalls were kept tidy by his staff of ranch hands. It smelled like hay and manure, like ranching, his life.

"She asked me to donate money for the new football uniforms, and then she told me to mention it to you. I didn't see why that was my job, so I told her—nicely, mind you— to call you herself."

"She's hitting you up for money, too?" What a relief. For a while there, he thought he was the only target for donations in town.

"I gave her a hundred bucks. Mostly to get her off my back."

"And that worked?"

"Sure did. Mom drilled it into my head over the years how important it is to chip in to fundraisers around town. But she also told me to set an annual budget for it and to not feel bad about saying no when the funds run out."

Smart woman. Mac doubted the same rules applied to him, though. His funds were practically limitless.

His funds? Make that Dad's funds.

It didn't feel right touching them.

"Are you going to the parade tomorrow?" Mac hoped he would say yes. If not, he'd have to watch with the rest of the guys, and as Blaine had mentioned, they all had girlfriends, wives or kids. Normally, it didn't bother him. But now?

His mind wandered back to Wednesday night and eating supper with Bridget. She'd looked so fresh and vibrant, and she got him in a way few did. When she'd said he was so much more than his money, he'd wanted to believe her.

He still wanted to believe her.

But he didn't.

"Nah," Blaine said. "I've got a lot of work to do around the ranch. If you've seen one Christmas parade, you've seen them all."

"Kaylee helped decorate the sophomores' float, so I'll be there." Had she been decorating it for other reasons, though? Like to see this Tanner kid?

"I heard Riley Sampson is setting up a coffee stand on the corner of Main and Third."

"Really?" He strode toward the offices at the end of the wide hallway separating the stalls. "Why would she do that? Bridget's place will be open all day."

Blaine shrugged. "Who knows? I never liked going in there much when Riley took over the shop, but maybe she's got a new brew or something."

"Yeah, I guess."

"I stopped into Brewed Awakening last week and got one of the double-espresso mochaccinos. Don't make fun of me. I needed caffeine, and it delivered. It rocked my world, really. Bridget's easy to be around. It's not hard to see why her shop is doing well."

Mac bristled. Did Blaine like Bridget or something?

"I'm not surprised, either. She knows her stuff."

"Randy told me Joe's been spending less time at the tackle shop now that he's working for Bridget. I teased him that he should give Bridget a bonus, but he got a funny look on his face. If I didn't know better, I'd say Randy misses having Joe around."

"Yeah, the last time I ran into Joe, we talked for a few minutes and *he* was the one who cut the conversation short. I didn't think much of it at the time, but it is a definite change from a few months ago. I actually enjoyed chatting with him."

"Maybe working there has him all talked out."

"Maybe." And maybe the fact Bridget treated Joe like a friend instead of a pest she needed to get rid of had made a difference.

A sliver of shame wiggled down his back as he thought

of how Bridget treated everyone with dignity. Could he say the same for himself?

He'd been avoiding a lot of people around town lately. Acting as if every request of theirs was a nuisance—and these were people who'd been good to him his entire life.

He needed to get his act together and figure out which causes to donate to before he became someone to avoid, too. He just didn't know how.

Maybe Bridget was on to something about donating where his heart was at.

He thought back to the idea her words had sparked. A phone call to Hannah's brother, Dr. David Carr, might clarify things.

Chapter Ten

Bridget peered out the front window of Brewed Awakening on Saturday morning. A crowd was gathering along the sidewalks in anticipation of the parade. And there, on the corner of Third Street, was Riley and her coffee/hot cocoa cart all decked out for Christmas. It looked like it had come straight out of a made-for-television movie. Bridget craned her neck to see if anyone was in line.

Yep. A woman was laughing as Riley handed her a small white cup, and several people stood behind her.

Bridget slunk away. She was counting on high sales today to add to her used-car fund and, hopefully, attract people who hadn't been here before. The coffee stand could give her some serious competition. But what could she do about it?

Either people liked Brewed Awakening or they didn't. To be fair, it might be more convenient to get their drinks from a stand today. Or they might miss having Riley as the coffee shop proprietor. It wasn't as if Bridget was all that chatty with customers. She preferred to listen, and oftentimes, they seemed to want to share their troubles with her. A few still acted suspicious when she sidestepped their probing questions, though.

If she kept thinking about Riley, she was going to give herself a headache. She plugged in the twinkle lights around the front window, then straightened the plaid bows on the wreaths nearby.

"Bridget?" Joe called from behind the counter. "I'm not seeing the reindeer stirrers. Am I looking in the wrong place?"

Bridget hustled back to the counter and found the box of brown plastic stirrers with reindeer faces as the bell clanged. She looked up to see an older couple stroll toward her with their grandson.

"Hi, Mr. and Mrs. Bloom. This must be Junior." She'd been working hard to learn people's names, and Shirley Bloom loved to talk about her seven-year-old grandson. Bridget leaned forward to speak to the boy. "Hey, there. Are you excited about the parade?"

"Yes!" Holding his grandmother's hand, he jumped up, his eyes sparkling. "Last year I got lots of candy. And I got to pet the horses after."

"Oh, wow." She grinned at him. "You must like horses."

"I do. Grandpa and I ride every weekend, don't we?" The kid was cute, she'd give him that.

The Blooms gave her their order, selected several baked goods and chatted with Joe briefly before leaving with their grandson skipping next to them.

No one else was in the shop.

Okay, so people obviously knew it was open. What had she done wrong? Bridget looked around—she'd worked so hard to make it festive and inviting.

Maybe the town liked Riley's coffee better than hers.

And maybe they liked Riley more, too. They might not really like Bridget all that much. Brewed Awakening was simply their last resort because they had nowhere else to get a cup of coffee.

"Well, Bridget, enjoy this while it lasts." Joe smiled at her, his eyes twinkling.

"No customers?" She hadn't meant to sound snarky, but what was she supposed to enjoy? No sales? Riley winning?

"The lull before the storm. It's about to get real busy."

She wanted to believe him but... "I don't understand why we're not busy now."

"Oh, don't worry about that." He waved dismissively. "People are still getting their spots. The ones who didn't bring their own coffees will want one soon. Once they're settled, they'll be sending a family member in with orders."

"Looks like they're sending the orders down to Riley's coffee stand." She hated sounding jealous. She hated *being* jealous.

"I've had her coffee." He grimaced. "It's better than nothing, but not much."

"Then why are they buying it?" She nibbled on her nail, realized what she was doing and forced herself to stop. This was getting ridiculous.

"Well, the Sampsons are well-liked around here. No one wants to snub her, because it would hurt her folks. You understand."

Yes, she did understand. Bridget understood perfectly well that she wasn't from around here. She didn't have folks people wouldn't want to hurt. And it was perfectly okay for them to snub her since she didn't count.

"Mark my words, this place will be full within the half hour."

"How can you be sure?"

"Easy. You make great coffee. And people like you."

His words slid down her core like rich, warm cocoa. Of all the kind things Joe had done for her, those words were needed the most.

"Thanks, Joe." She gave him a quick hug. "I needed to hear that."

"It's the truth." He nodded sternly.

"You're a good friend."

"I am?" He seemed genuinely perplexed, and his face grew red.

"Of course." She gave him a smile. It hit her that maybe she wasn't the only one who wasn't sure of her status in town. Did Joe feel like an outsider at times, too? Even though he'd lived here his entire life? "How many afternoons have you stayed to help me out when you didn't have to? And all these Saturdays? You've really been there for me, and I, well, I enjoy having you around. I don't know what I'd do without you."

"You're a good friend, too." He looked a bit choked up. The bell clanged, and Bridget turned to see who was coming in. To her surprise, a large group of people entered. She inwardly grinned. Joe was right. It had been the lull before the storm.

Hopefully, the storm would bring in new customers and a flood of sales.

"Welcome to Brewed Awakening…"

"I wish you could have seen the parade." Kaylee addressed Bridget as she took a seat at the counter near closing time.

Mac sat next to her. It had been a long but fun day. After the parade, he'd taken Kaylee and Lydia out to lunch, then around all the shops. They'd bought some Christmas presents and stopped by the high school to walk around the holiday art fair. When Lydia left with her parents, he and Kaylee had decided a coffee break was necessary.

As usual, he couldn't look away from the beauty behind

the counter. This desire to see Bridget, to spend time with her, was getting too strong for him to ignore.

"Our float was awesome. And Tanner was my partner to throw candy to the kids."

"He was?" Bridget raised her eyebrows and leaned in. "Anything new I should know about?"

Mac tried to look like he wasn't eavesdropping.

"No." Kaylee looked down shyly. "He texted me last night to see where Lydia and I were meeting this morning, though."

"See? That's something." Bridget nodded briskly. "It won't be long before he starts texting you all the time. Wait—" she snapped her fingers "—do you have any high school dances coming up?"

"No." Kaylee stuck her bottom lip out. "Bummer, huh."

"Yeah." Bridget looked disappointed.

Not in his book. This was his little sister. The girl he gave piggyback rides to and taught how to ride a horse. She wasn't old enough to date. She wasn't ready.

Or maybe he wasn't ready.

"All day I've heard a lot of compliments about your singing." Bridget straightened the few remaining cookies on the tray next to him. Mac liked watching her fingers move—everything she did had a purpose.

"From who?" Kaylee straightened.

"Members of the choir. One even suggested you should do a solo."

Mac was taken aback. Kaylee? A solo? He doubted she'd be up for it.

"A solo?" she said breathlessly. "Really?"

She looked excited, not worried. Hmm.

"Really." Bridget grinned.

"That would be amazing. But…" She winced. "I don't know."

Mac cleared his throat. "Even if they ask you, you don't have to say yes."

"True," Kaylee replied. Was he imagining it or did she seem to shrink at his words?

"Or you could say yes." Bridget nodded brightly before sending a glare his way. What was that look for?

"I could, couldn't I?"

The front door opened and Joe Schlock walked in. "Are you almost ready?"

"I sure am. Will you give me a few minutes?" Bridget beamed at the man.

"Take your time," Joe said. "Want me to lock the front door?"

"Yes, please."

"Oh, hey, Mac. Kaylee." Joe flipped the Open sign to Closed and turned the deadbolt. "Did you enjoy the parade? I heard your class's float was a hit with all those snowmen."

"It was fun." Kaylee swiveled on the stool and smiled. "We thought one of the snowmen's heads was going to fall off for a minute, but Ginger held on to it. I don't know what would have happened if it wasn't for her. Oh, by the way, I saved you these." She reached into her pocket and pulled out two suckers.

"How did you know cherry's my favorite?" His eyes twinkled as he accepted them.

"I had a hunch." She winked. "What are you and Bridget doing?"

Yes, Mac wondered the same. He knew Bridget thought a lot of Joe, but he hadn't realized they spent time together outside of work.

"Joe, here, is taking me to his buddy's place to look at a used car." Bridget, positively glowing, hurried back to them. "And since everyone in town came in today to buy coffees and treats, I'm feeling much better about my prospects of having my own vehicle soon."

"Oh, wow, that's great!" Kaylee clapped her hands. "Did you get your license yet?"

"I haven't." Bridget turned her attention to Mac, causing his veins to thrum with energy. "I'm hoping I can sneak in some more driving time this week during choir practice. If you're up for it?"

He was up for it.

But he also wasn't.

He was spending so much time with her. His feelings weren't neutral—they were overheated—and being in a small space together, his truck, wasn't helping. Every time she drove, he'd catch a whiff of her perfume. And his heart would thump when she gave him that wry smile of hers. He'd reach over and touch her hand to direct her attention to something, and his hand always wanted to linger.

"Yeah, I'm up for it," he said gruffly. Then he turned to Kaylee. "And you, why don't you drive us home? Let Joe and Bridget wrap things up?"

"Okay."

Wait…had she just agreed to drive? He'd barely gotten her to drive more than a mile this week.

"Why aren't you fighting me on this?"

She blinked up at him. "I need to get my license. What if Tanner asks me to meet him at the Barking Squirrel or something?"

"Tanner? You're getting your license for a guy?" He'd done everything he could to ease her into driving, and this Tanner kid was the reason she was finally willing to learn?

"It doesn't matter why you're getting your license," Bridget said. "The important thing is that you're getting some driving practice."

Well, this was great. Now Mac was going to worry

about her being on the road *and* some high school punk putting the moves on her.

"All set back here." Joe breezed in from the back room with Bridget's coat in his hand. She took it from him and put it on. The four of them headed to the entrance.

"I hope you find a car." Kaylee waved.

"Me too." Bridget shrugged happily. "See you Monday."

He and Kaylee headed to the truck. He should be happy. Bridget would get a car. She'd get her license. There'd be no reason for them to spend all this time together anymore. And Kaylee was on track to eventually get her license. She'd be able to drive herself home, which would free up his afternoons to get more done on the ranch.

His life would go back to normal.

But what if he didn't want it to?

"Hop in." He sighed.

First things first. Surviving Kaylee driving them home.

The Tuesday before Christmas, Bridget could barely contain her excitement. The past two weeks had flown by in a flurry of Christmas prep. *Come on, Mac, get here already!* She couldn't wait to tell him her big news.

Kaylee had choir practice and had asked Bridget to make a peppermint mocha for Mac to pick up for her before closing the shop for the night. When Bridget thought of Kaylee, she couldn't help but smile. The girl had been asked to sing "To Shepherds as They Watched by Night" for the Christmas Eve service, and Bridget was thrilled when she'd agreed.

Kaylee had taught Bridget how to harmonize with her while they closed every Monday and Wednesday. Sometimes Mac would be waiting and would join them, too.

His voice did something to Bridget's heart. As did his clear love for Jesus when he sang. And the fact he was willing to sing with Kaylee to make her feel more comfortable about having a solo? What guy did that?

Mac was a good man. She'd known it for some time. It was getting harder to ignore her feelings for him. Especially since they'd spent so many hours together driving while Kaylee was at practice. Enough hours to give Bridget the confidence to make the appointment she'd gone to this afternoon.

The front door opened and a gust of wind blew in snow around Mac. He shivered as he shut the door behind him, then he looked up and met her eyes. The gray flashed to silver. They had a gleam she wouldn't even pretend to deny.

He enjoyed seeing her as much as she did him.

Inhaling a shaky breath, she rounded the counter to greet him.

"I have Kaylee's peppermint mocha ready. I made something for you, too—honey graham. Decaf." She stopped a foot away from him, aware of how tall he was, the smoothness of his shaved jaw and the broadness of his chest.

"Good, I need my beauty sleep."

"Sure, you do." She shook her head playfully. She couldn't wait a minute longer. She had to show him what she'd gotten earlier. Whipping the small card out of her pocket, she held it up to him. "I did it!"

He squinted as he studied the card. Then his lips curved into a wide grin. "Congratulations!"

To her shock, he wrapped his arms around her and lifted her off the ground in a half circle before setting her on her feet and taking a step back.

"Thanks, Mac, I don't know how I could possibly ever thank you enough." Holding her driver's license in her hand filled her with the best feeling. She had the freedom to drive. Independence. She could go anywhere. Do anything.

But being in his arms just now? Even better.

"You can officially drive." He let his fingers trail down the back of her hand. "How does it feel?"

Feel? All she could feel was his tender touch. And she wanted him to pick her up and twirl her again. To feel those strong arms around her.

"It feels amazing." She tucked her license back in her pocket.

"You worked hard for it. And you're definitely ready to get out there on your own. You've got more confidence now."

"All because of you. I couldn't have done it without you." She gazed into his eyes, and her breath caught at the intensity in them. This chemistry they shared had been simmering for a while. With every new insight she learned about him, she wanted to be around him even more.

"You're welcome." The words came out low, so low she leaned in. She wondered if he wanted to kiss her. It sure seemed like he did.

It had been ages since she'd been kissed. If she could have one thing right now in this moment, it would be his lips on hers.

As if he could read her mind, he bent his head and kissed her.

It was like a Christmas dream. The minty taste of his lips brought a tingle to hers. She relaxed into the gentle strength of his arms around her. As she kissed him back, the sensation of being special, being the one Mac thought was special, filled her with headiness.

For the briefest moment she had the feeling this was exactly why she'd moved to Sunrise Bend.

For this kiss.

This man supported her but didn't cage her in.

Bridget stepped away abruptly, bringing her hand to

her mouth. She was playing a dangerous game, one she couldn't bear to lose.

Mac only saw what she'd chosen to show him. He didn't know the truth.

"What's wrong?" Doubts circled in his eyes—along with insecurity. Could he feel insecure, too? Impossible. Not him.

"Nothing," she said brightly. "It's been a while since I've kissed anyone."

"It's been a while for me, too." The raw honesty in his gaze made her want to take a chance and share some of the secrets in her past, but she could only stare. He traced his finger down her cheek. "Did someone break your heart?"

"My stepmother." The words were out before she could lock them in. She winced. "Sorry, that came out wrong."

"I was thinking more along the lines of a boyfriend." The corner of his mouth quirked.

"Yeah, I know." She backed up another step, rubbing her forearms. "No, I haven't gotten serious with anyone."

"Really? You?" He looked surprised. "I haven't either."

"Why not?"

"I'm complicated."

"How so?"

"Live in the shadow of your father long enough, and you become a shadow." He grabbed the coffees she'd set out. "Forget I said anything."

"Mac, wait." She grabbed his arm. "You're not a shadow. You're solid. Real." She stared up into his eyes. "You're the most solid man I've ever known."

His eyes shimmered as he stepped toward her once more. He reached around and set the cups on the counter, then eased his hand behind her neck and drew her to him, kissing her slowly, thoroughly, as if he wanted to savor every moment.

She'd be savoring the memory later that night.

When he ended the kiss, he moved his hands to her lower back. "What did your stepmother do to break your heart?" His voice was husky.

Frost chilled her from his words. What didn't her stepmother do would be the better question. After Bridget's father died, she'd been little more than a servant. She'd spent her adolescence riddled with anxiety from being told she was worthless every day. She'd been separated from her friends, taken out of the school she loved and emotionally abused by her stepmother and stepsister.

No one had cared. No one had seen what was happening. No one had rescued her.

Bridget tried to push away the bad memories. Her early teen years had been a nightmare she'd been trying her best to forget.

"She wasn't a kind woman." She didn't want to discuss it. "What about you? Why haven't you gotten serious with anyone?"

He massaged the back of his neck, looking like he had no clue how to answer. "Haven't met the right person, I guess."

She wasn't buying it. From his expression, she was certain he knew exactly why he'd avoided having a serious girlfriend. Clearly, they both had things in their pasts they wanted to hide.

"You better take these. They'll get cold, and Kaylee will wonder where you're at." She handed him the coffees, wishing the warmth of his kiss could have lingered.

He hesitated, clearly wanting to say something else, but he didn't. "I'll see you later then."

She followed him to the front door.

"What are you doing for Christmas?" he asked before opening it.

"I'm having lunch at Sawyer and Tess's."

"What about Christmas Eve?"

"Well, obviously I'll be at the Christmas Eve service to listen to Kaylee sing."

"Come to my house after. We'll have a fire and hang out. The three of us. I can take you home later."

"I'd love that, but I'll drive myself. I'm getting my new ride tonight. Joe and I are picking it up. It's an older model SUV with low miles. He has a friend in a nearby town whose wife no longer drives, so they decided to sell it. I got a really good deal."

"That's great." His smile couldn't get any wider. "So you'll come over after the service? It's hard to believe Christmas Eve is this Friday already."

"Yeah, I'll be there." She locked gazes with him for a long moment. Then he left.

Christmas Eve with Mac and Kaylee. She couldn't imagine a better way to spend the holiday. Sooner or later, though, she was going to have to either fill Mac in about the reality of her teen years or distance herself from him.

Eventually, he'd want to know more about her past, and if she told him, he might be embarrassed to find out how she'd been forced to live. Even if he wasn't, he was sure to view her differently—pity her—which would be just as painful.

Making tough decisions was part of life, though. She owed it to him to tell him the truth.

Chapter Eleven

The wind kicked up as Mac checked the time Thursday afternoon. Almost time to drive Kaylee into town for her final choir practice. Tomorrow was Christmas Eve, and he was looking forward to having Bridget over after church. In fact, ever since he'd kissed her on Tuesday, he hadn't been able to get that kiss off his mind. He'd found the perfect gift for her, too.

Just because Dad had claimed women would walk all over him didn't mean it would automatically come true.

Part of him wasn't sure, though.

He urged Caesar back over the ridge. He'd been looking for a missing calf for the past two hours. Mac really didn't want to leave right now—not until he knew the calf was safe. He'd just check beyond the ridge. It wouldn't take long.

With a dusting of snow on the ground and the sky a pale gray, he burrowed his chin into his scarf as Caesar crested the ridge. Mac scanned the area. Two small herds of cattle were grazing with stragglers between them. One of those calves could be the one he was looking for.

The horse snorted as he motioned it forward. Soon, he was near the main group, searching for the correct tag.

Disappointment hit him when he realized it wasn't there. He moved on to the other group of cattle, slowly taking in each number, looking for the cows the missing calf typically stayed around. Nothing.

Calves didn't vanish into thin air. He frowned, uncertain where to look next. Could it have wandered off and been attacked? Maybe one of the ranch hands had found it.

His phone rang. He winced. He'd lost track of time. It was probably Kaylee wanting to know where he was.

"Hello?"

"Hi, Mac." Bridget's voice hit him square in the chest. "Are you guys on your way?"

"No." He checked the time. They were really going to be late. "I've been looking for a calf."

"Oh, I was worried. Kaylee told me she'd stop in first for a hot tea with honey, and when I didn't see her…"

"I'll go back to the house right now." Only then did he realize how cold he was. "I've got to ride back to the stables first, though, and put Caesar away."

"Okay, see you in a little bit."

"Yeah." He noticed all the texts that had come through. The last one was from Kaylee. He opened it.

I don't feel good. I'm skipping practice.

His stomach soured. She'd been doing so well for the past two months. Was it a headache? A cold? The flu?

He called her. "What's going on?"

"My head hurts."

"You have a fever? Sore throat? Feel like you're going to puke?"

"No."

The relief hitting him felt out of proportion to the conversation. "Okay, what's wrong then? Did something happen?"

He tightened his grip on the phone. Maybe this Tanner kid had hurt her feelings. They'd been talking and texting each other a lot lately.

"No. I just don't feel up to it."

"The choir's counting on you, Kay." They wouldn't be thrilled with her if she skipped the final practice.

"I can't go, okay?" She sounded upset, which made him upset, and he thought about the missing calf and the presents he still needed to wrap and the calls he still needed to make to Dina Jones and John Lutz and all the other people who were hoping he'd donate money.

All of it was giving him a headache, too.

"Okay," Mac said. "Put an ice pack on your head. Maybe that will help." Even as he said it, he had a bad feeling. Like he was doing the wrong thing. He could picture Bridget's glare, and it made him squirm.

"Thanks, Mac."

That's when he remembered he'd told Bridget they'd be there soon. "Listen, Kay, do me a favor and let Bridget know you're not coming. She called just now worried you hadn't shown up, and I'm out here trying to find a calf…"

"I'll call her," she said quietly. The line went dead.

Problem solved. He could find the calf, Kaylee could get some rest, and when he finished up, he'd finally make some decisions about the donations.

It was time. It was past time.

Being around Bridget for the past weeks had changed him. She made him not only want more out of life, but also made him believe he was up to the challenges his father hadn't trusted him with. He was falling hard for Bridget, and a large reason why was her respect for him.

But would she still respect him when she found out he'd let Kaylee skip practice?

* * *

"What do you mean you're skipping practice?" Bridget had closed the shop for the night and gone upstairs to her apartment after calling Mac earlier. She stared in disbelief at her Christmas tree with its pretty twinkling lights.

"I don't feel up to it."

"Well, I don't always feel up to doing things, either, but I still do them."

"You're different."

"Did something happen with Tanner?"

"No. He's been really nice to me."

"Then what is going on?"

"I have a headache."

She inhaled and counted to three. Headache or not, Kaylee could push through for one practice, couldn't she? Didn't the girl realize how good she had it here? Everyone liked her. But if she couldn't be counted on to follow through with her commitments, would they turn on her?

"Kaylee, the church choir is counting on you. It's not right to let them down."

"My head hurts!" She sounded shrill. Bridget wasn't arguing about it, but she had the feeling Kaylee was just making excuses. Maybe her head really did hurt, but something more was going on.

"And Mac's okay with this?"

"Yes. He told me to get an ice pack."

Of course, he did.

Bridget had an entire list of things she'd like to say to him at this moment. Like why don't you stand up and be firm with your sister? Letting her slink away from a commitment wasn't helping her.

"If I come pick you up, will you at least go and practice your solo one more time? I can take you right home. It wouldn't be long."

Silence.

"Please?" Bridget wasn't one to beg, but Kaylee was too important to her. She didn't want her to be whispered about. She didn't want people looking down on her. She didn't want her to have regrets.

"Why?" Kaylee asked quietly. "Why is it important to you?"

Bridget's throat tightened. "Because *you're* important to me. I know how much you love to sing, and I know how hard you've practiced the song. I want you to have this, Kaylee. For you."

A few seconds ticked by.

"I'll go. Just for my solo."

Relief almost brought tears to her eyes. Why was she so worked up? "I'll leave right now. Tell Mac I'm taking you."

Bridget hung up and raced down the stairwell to her SUV. She'd driven it a few times already. It wasn't as top-of-the-line as Mac's truck, but she was getting used to it. After checking her mirrors, she backed out and drove to their ranch.

After she pulled up near their house, she texted Kaylee.

With her winter coat wide open, Kaylee hurried to the SUV and got into the passenger side. Her normally bright face was pinched. Bridget began the return trip to town and tried to make conversation, but she only got mono-syllabic answers.

Maybe Kaylee really did have a bad headache. Had Bridget been wrong to insist she attend the practice?

After a silent drive, she pulled into the church parking lot and accompanied Kaylee inside. They hung up their coats, then Bridget slipped into a seat in the back, and Kaylee shuffled to the front. The choir was singing "Joy to the World."

When the song ended, one of the middle-aged moms

pointed Kaylee to the microphone up front. She trudged to the mic, adjusted it and stared unseeing ahead.

The opening chords of the song began to play, and Kaylee started to sing. Her sweet voice filled the church, and everyone there watched her in rapt attention. Bridget was tempted to hum the harmonization, but she remained silent.

Lord, thank You for blessing Kaylee with a beautiful voice. And thank You for giving her the desire to share it with this church.

A choking sound startled her. Kaylee began to jog down the center aisle with tears streaming down her face. Bridget ran to meet her. "What's wrong? Are you sick?"

She shook her head, her face flushed and wet with tears. "I want to go home, and if you won't take me, I'll call Mac. I just want to go home!"

Bridget widened her eyes and met the choir director's gaze. The woman nodded to her in sympathy. Bridget put her arm around Kaylee's shoulders and led her to their coats.

"I'm sorry, Kaylee. Of course, I'll take you home right now."

After bundling up, they got back into her SUV, and Bridget began the drive home. The sky had grown dark, so she turned on the headlights and tried to focus on the road. Kaylee sobbed softly in the passenger seat for a few minutes, and Bridget felt helpless.

And guilty. So guilty.

"I'm sorry." She'd do anything to take away her pain. "If you want to talk…"

Kaylee shook her head rapidly.

It was a long ride back to the ranch.

When she pulled into the drive and parked the vehicle, Kaylee practically jumped out of the car and raced to the porch. Bridget got out, too. She had to speak to Mac about this.

But her heart had grown jagged edges, because she already knew what he was going to say to her.

She'd pushed Kaylee too hard.

And she couldn't deny it.

She regretted it and probably always would.

Chapter Twelve

Mac heard the front door slam and looked up from the documents he'd been poring over in the den. One of the ranch hands had found the calf safe and sound a while ago. Since then, Mac had been reviewing all the quotes he'd been given for the various projects he'd been asked to fund. He got up, setting the papers on the large desk, and went out to investigate.

"Kaylee?" he called, but he didn't see her. Another door slam coming from the direction of her room alerted him she was definitely home.

The front door opened slightly, and Bridget's face peeked in. "Can I come in?"

"Yeah, what's going on?" He tried to think of what could have happened and came up blank.

"I'm not sure." She took two steps into the hall and halted. The questions running through her eyes filled him with dread.

"Did she get sick?"

"I don't think so," she said quietly. "I mean, I knew she didn't want to go to practice when she called me. And I told her I'd pick her up—to at least practice her solo one more time—and she agreed."

He curled his fingers into his palms. Kaylee hadn't told him any of that. She'd simply texted him that Bridget was taking her and she'd be home later. He'd assumed Kaylee did her typical about-face as soon as Bridget was involved. Clearly, he'd assumed wrong.

"What. Happened?" His legs were rooted in place.

"She was quiet all the way there. And when she went up front she seemed fine." Bridget got a faraway look in her eye. "She began to sing, and her voice is so pure, Mac, so beautiful—"

"What. Happened?" His muscles tensed, and he had half a mind to march down the hall to Kaylee's room and ask her himself.

"She made a choking sound, and then the next thing I know she's running down the aisle. Crying."

Crying? Why was Kaylee crying?

"Do you know why?"

"No." Bridget stared at the ground. "She wouldn't tell me."

His frustration reached a boiling point.

"So let me get this straight." He skewered her with his gaze. "You went behind my back and told Kaylee she had to go to practice after I told her she could stay home? What part of "she had a headache" didn't you understand?"

Bridget's chin raised a notch. "I understood she had a headache. I also understood she's used it as an excuse to avoid uncomfortable situations in the past."

"Or maybe she just had a headache. Did you think of that?" He was getting too worked up. He hadn't felt this angry in years.

"No. I didn't." Her words were soft, and her gaze never left his. "I still don't."

He turned away, putting his fist to his mouth and blowing, before addressing her again. "Kaylee isn't tough like you, okay? She's fifteen. A kid. This will probably set her back for months."

"Fifteen isn't that young, Mac. And she may not be tough like me—whatever that means—but she can handle more than you think."

"You're from New York. You lived on your own. You're older, more mature. You have no idea what she's going through."

"What is she going through?" Her small voice only infuriated him more.

He didn't know.

He didn't know what she was going through because she never told him. She seemed to tell Bridget everything, though.

"You tell me." Mac pointed to her. "She confides in you an awful lot."

"Not this."

He'd been wanting to give Kaylee a nice Christmas, and this likely ruined it for her.

"I can't believe you would be this heartless," he said coldly. "I'm tired of you pushing Kaylee past her limits. You walked all over both of us today. It won't happen again."

This was turning into a nightmare, and it was all her fault.

Mac was right. Bridget had no authority to tell Kaylee to go to practice. She should have minded her own business. What did it matter to her if Kaylee skipped or not?

It mattered.

A lot.

She cared about Kaylee and wanted her teen years to be better than her own.

And Mac had every right to yell at her. She'd grown so close to him and Kaylee that she'd overstepped her bounds.

"You're right." Bridget licked her lips, forcing herself

to look in his eyes, to let him see the truth in hers. "I was heartless. I never should have pushed Kaylee tonight. I should have been more patient, shouldn't have overridden you."

A shift in his eyes told her he was listening. The set of his jaw didn't bode well, though.

"What you see isn't what you get when you look at me. I'm not like everyone around here. You said I was tough. I guess I've been tough since I was twelve years old. After my father died, my stepmother had custody of me. She didn't like me. I was immediately taken out of the private school I'd been attending and enrolled in an online school. My stepsister still went to the private academy, though. I basically became a servant. My stepmother was emotionally abusive."

She forced herself to keep staring into his eyes, even as his look shifted from anger to concern. "When I was sixteen, she kicked me out. I had nothing but a backpack full of clothes and fifty bucks I stole from my stepsister."

Mac's jaw dropped, and she took it as a sign to keep going before she lost her nerve.

"I had nowhere to go. No friends. My stepmother flat out told me if I went to child services, they would send me right back to her, and she'd tell them I had anger issues. That's all it took for me to kill that idea. The first couple of nights on the streets were the worst. I was too afraid to sleep. The money ran out quick."

He was shaking his head, disgusted.

Why wouldn't he be? He didn't even know the worst of it.

She had to tell him everything. Every ugly little thing about her life back then.

"I couldn't get a job. No high school diploma. For the record, I never earned my diploma. I do have a GED, thanks to Sawyer's help. I spent my time wandering around the city. I went to food banks, but I knew better than to linger there for long. Too many questions. Too many ways for them to send me back to her. So, I climbed into dumpsters for food."

He shook his head again.

"I walked a lot at night. Took naps during the day. It was summer. I didn't sleep much because I had to be on alert all the time." She swallowed hard, thinking about the two occasions she'd been grabbed by strange men. She'd screamed, fought them with everything she had and managed to escape both times.

"Sawyer was working at a diner, and he saw me in the alley. He gave me some food and told me to come back the next day. So, I did. And every day after that. He told me he could get me a job. I couldn't tell him I didn't even have an address to put on an application, but he seemed to know I had no place to go. The next day when I came around, he introduced me to a woman in her early sixties. Said she'd helped him when he was in a bind and she'd help me, too."

Bridget didn't even attempt to decipher Mac's expression.

"I'd been on the streets for almost two months at that point. I was desperate and thankful. I slept on her couch for a while. Worked at the diner, too. Sawyer lived next door to her. When the apartment across from him became available, he helped me with the deposit. I don't know what would have happened to me if I hadn't met him."

Mac closed his eyes as if he was in pain. "Bridget…"

"I'm not done—" she scrunched her nose "—so don't say anything. I'm sorry for letting you think I'm someone I'm not. The truth is I was homeless, ate food out of garbage cans, didn't shower for two months, never finished high school and was a fool to ever think I could be someone new here. You're an amazing guy, Mac, and I'm just…trash." A tear slid down her cheek. "Please tell Kaylee I'm sorry."

She turned to go, but Mac stopped her. "Wait, you can't leave after telling me all that."

"There's nothing more to say." She flicked the tears away.

"Nothing more to say?" he bellowed. "I don't understand why you didn't tell me. We've spent a lot of time together. Shared a lot, Bridget. Didn't you think you could trust me?"

"It wasn't about trust."

"Then what was it about?"

"I fell in love with you, Mac. I love you, and I'm not the right woman for you. I never was." She couldn't stand here another minute. She opened the door, and Mac caught it. "Please, Mac, just let me go."

He blinked as if in pain, and she slipped outside, pulling her coat tightly around her body as she made her way to the SUV.

Hadn't she known all along a relationship with him would never work?

She slid the key into the ignition and glanced at the porch. He stood in the doorway, the Christmas lights all around him, and didn't move. She put the SUV in Reverse and headed out of there.

So much for keeping a low profile, avoiding romance with one of the town's single ranchers.

She'd put her future at risk, and the worst thing was that she didn't even care. If she lost the coffee shop, she'd survive. But losing Mac? Losing Kaylee?

Bridget didn't know how to face a future without them.

Chapter Thirteen

He didn't deserve her.

When Bridget's vehicle drove out of view, Mac closed the front door and hung his head. The numbness he'd been feeling while she'd told him about her past was beginning to thaw out, sending a prickly sensation through his veins the same as if he'd been out in the cold too long. The straightforward *just the facts* way she'd shared her past with him had kept him silent.

He didn't know how to process it.

"Mac?" Kaylee came up behind him.

He almost jumped. Whirling to her, he exhaled. "Yeah?"

"I overheard you and Bridget. And I came out here to tell you it wasn't her fault about today, and I didn't mean to eavesdrop, but I heard everything she said, and…" A growly sound ripped from her throat. "I can't believe she went through all that. I feel so bad."

She threw her arms around him and began to cry. He couldn't believe it either. He felt bad, too. As Kaylee's shoulders shook, his tangled thoughts slowly began to make sense.

Bridget had been tossed out when she was practically a kid.

How could he have called her heartless? Why hadn't he given her the benefit of the doubt?

Her heart was bigger than he'd ever given her credit for. Big enough to hire his sister. Big enough to befriend Joe Schlock. Big enough to drive all the way out here today to help Kaylee honor her commitment.

She hadn't walked all over him or Kaylee.

He'd been the one to walk all over her.

Bridget had told him she loved him. He'd almost overlooked those three little words, but they came back, echoing in his mind.

She didn't think she was the right woman for him.

Him. The guy whose father had undermined him his entire life. The guy who'd been playing it safe relationship-wise because he couldn't face becoming what his dad predicted. A wimp. A complete pushover when it came to women.

Sixteen… Bridget had been kicked out at sixteen… Homeless… Nowhere to go.

He hated that. Hated she'd been treated so shamefully. Hated she'd been forced out on the streets. Hated she'd had to fend for herself against who knew what.

He couldn't even begin to think about what that might be.

"Mac?" Kaylee looked up at him, her eyes damp and red.

"What?"

"You're upset, aren't you?"

He realized he was squeezing her too hard and loosened his hold. "No…well… I'm upset that you're upset."

"I know you are." She let go of him and led the way to the family room. Then she sank into the couch, pulling a fluffy throw over her legs and up to her chin. "Bridget was right."

"About what?" He sat in a chair kitty-corner from her.

"I do love to sing."

Then why did she want to skip practice today?

"For the past couple of months, I've felt more myself again. I like it here." Kaylee wore a wistful expression. "And I thought singing in the choir would honor Mom's memory."

"It does."

"Tomorrow's Christmas Eve, and I thought I'd be okay. I thought I'd be able to sing, but every time the first words come out, all I can think of is how much I miss her, how she and I should be making cookies and watching movies and all the things we used to do. My throat tightens and I burst into tears. I can't sing tomorrow. I just can't."

He should have known—should have guessed it. Why hadn't he realized how tough the holidays were going to be without her mom and their dad?

"You've been doing so good," Mac said gently. "Ever since you started working at the coffee shop, you've been your old self again. I like seeing you smile. It's a relief to see you happy."

"I love working there. I don't think about things so much when I'm making the coffees and talking to Bridget. She's really easy to talk to. She gets me."

Mac knew it was true.

"I know you think she forced me to go today." Kaylee glanced at him. "It wasn't like that, though. I'm important to her. That's why she pushed me. She said she wanted me to go for me."

"Maybe you need a break from the choir. Or a distraction. Then you won't hurt so much."

"I don't want a distraction." Her voice rose. "I don't want to take my mind off it. I think I need to stop pushing it all away. I need to feel sad and miss Mom. I think every nerve in my body is aching to remember her and what we had. I need to mourn."

"But I don't want you to be in pain."

"Pain is part of it, though." Kaylee looked genuinely surprised. "I loved Mom more than anyone—and I loved Dad, too, Mac. It's just…he wasn't around much. Mom and I spent all our time together, so I miss her more. And if I wasn't sad right now, don't you think it would be weird? When you love someone, you miss them, you feel sad they're not around. The thought of never seeing them or talking to them or hugging them again is hard. It's just so hard. I've been trying to avoid the pain for months, and I can't avoid it anymore, and I don't think I want to. I want to feel it."

He studied her. There was peace under her sadness. She looked stronger than he'd ever seen her.

Kaylee dropped her gaze to her lap, then looked at him. "I get it now. Why Bridget is always willing to listen, so easy to talk to. I feel really bad. Like losing Mom and Dad was horrible, but I got to come live with you. I didn't have to sleep on the streets and climb into a dumpster for food. It's why she has so much sympathy—or empathy— I never know which is which. She's just compassionate, you know?"

Yeah, he did know. And he'd accused her of terrible things.

He'd been wrong about Bridget, and it looked like he'd been wrong about Kaylee, too.

Was there anything he was right about?

Teardrops were spilling onto her cheeks again as she stared out the back windows. He wanted to tell her not to cry, that she didn't have to sing or do anything. He'd put on a goofy Christmas movie, attempt to bake cookies— anything, anything to take away the pain.

But he realized she was right. She needed to mourn, and he'd have to get used to her being sad at times instead of trying to make it all better.

He went over to her and gave her another hug. Then he sat next to her and held her for a long while. When she was done crying, he asked her to tell him everything she missed about her mom.

And she did.

For the next hour, they shared memories of Jeanette and their larger-than-life father, laughing at some of his favorite expressions, feeling sad about his misplaced priorities.

When they were talked out, Kaylee excused herself to her room, and he sat there staring at the towering, professionally decorated Christmas tree. It brought to mind putting Bridget's tree up at her place, the apartment she thought was so luxurious—now he knew why.

A profound sense of shame came over him. Bridget loved Kaylee. She'd gone out of her way to help his sister, and she'd given her the confidence needed to attend school every day, to go to driver's ed classes, to not give up when life got hard.

She'd brought Kaylee's smile back.

And he, on the other hand, had only given his sister free passes to avoid her problems instead of dealing with them.

The truth was, he'd been molding Kaylee to be weak. He'd had little confidence in her ability to handle her problems. Worse, he'd lashed out at Bridget the way his dad had done to him countless times. It had always been his father's way or the highway.

And he was disgusted to recognize he'd treated Bridget the same.

Instead of becoming a doormat, he'd been a bulldozer.

He didn't like what he'd become.

* * *

After a tense drive home from Mac's, Bridget let herself into her apartment. Flicking on the lights, she inhaled the homey scents. Cinnamon and vanilla and old wood floors. Setting her small purse on the counter, she took off her coat and padded through the kitchen to the living room, then crouched to plug in her tree. The white lights flashed on, and she took them in for a long moment before sitting on the couch and curling her legs under her.

A strange emptiness loomed inside her. She'd thought her heart would break when she left Mac's, but it was as if her heart had left her body altogether. A pin could drop in her innermost being and she'd likely be able to hear the clatter when it landed.

There was nothing left to feel.

Maybe there'd never been anything to feel. Her hot emotions had been frozen and beaten down many times in her childhood. Having a mentally unstable stepmother did that to a person. After meeting Sawyer, it had taken a full year for her not to panic at random times with the fear of losing her apartment or not having anything to eat. As time wore on, she'd slowly gotten back to a more normal frame of mind.

Moving here had been the biggest leap of faith she'd ever made. She'd bought into the fantasy that she could have a more complete life in Sunrise Bend. Her own business, Sawyer and Tess as friends, a sense of community.

She'd never dared think she could have a boyfriend, too.

And, yet, she'd grown close to Mac. Very close.

She'd been allowing herself too many dreams.

Bridget tucked a soft throw over her lap. Why hadn't she kept her mouth shut when Kaylee called earlier? It wasn't her place to push the girl, and it definitely wasn't her place to override Mac's judgment.

She'd just wanted to help. Wanted Kaylee to overcome whatever was bothering her.

And she'd made it ten times worse.

Usually when people had problems, she listened and didn't spout off a bunch of advice she wasn't qualified to give. But it had felt different with Kaylee. She'd seen so much suffering in her—suffering Bridget understood—and she'd wanted to give her strength. To let her know she'd make it through the pain.

Bridget had been afraid for her, too. Afraid the town would turn on her. But instead of protecting Kaylee, all Bridget had done was given her the final nudge to fall apart.

No wonder Mac said she was heartless.

She'd learned her lesson. She never should have pressured Kaylee. And she never should have fallen in love with Mac. He knew the truth about her now. There was no going back.

Past midnight Mac slumped on the couch and stared at the Christmas tree, feeling as dejected as he could remember. He'd tried to watch television, tried to go to sleep, tried to silence the chaos in his mind, but he'd failed at everything. So here he was, ready to face the truth.

The only person who'd walked all over Mac was his father. The man had never seen the best in his son, never understood him and never wanted to.

And it was one of the reasons Mac had bent over backward to make Kaylee comfortable here. Because if he'd started barking out orders and throwing his weight around like Dad did, she would have resented him.

Kaylee was his family. The only family he had left.

Lord, I messed up. I couldn't see straight with Kaylee. I'm glad she's smart enough to realize she needs to grieve. I shouldn't have tried to take that away from her.

Deep down, he knew she'd be okay. They'd have a talk soon about expectations. What she needed from him. What he needed from her.

Bridget had been right to encourage the best parts of her. Kaylee was much stronger than he'd thought.

Maybe Kaylee was onto something about needing to feel the pain. He'd been avoiding his own for years, putting it off, hoping it would go away.

It had only festered.

Dad was gone, and Mac hadn't become the pushover he'd predicted, even if he had been acting like an idiot lately. Avoiding hard talks with Kaylee, avoiding the people around town, avoiding dealing with the inheritance.

Maybe Mac resented the money. What it represented. His father had cared more about making a profit than about his own son. But Dad had loved him in his own warped way.

Mac had always wanted a different kind of father.

The lights on the tree glowed as his mind quieted.

The truth was he had a different kind of father.

Lord, You're the Father I need. You always have been. You're the One who accepts me for who I am. The One who gave me the courage to ask Dad to move here as a teen. The One who blessed me with good friends and a job I love.

Emotion coursed through him as he thought of all the ways God had upheld him after he'd moved here. All the people God had sent his way to encourage him, to include him, to help him.

I'm sorry, Lord. I am sorry. He dropped his forehead into his hands as regrets hit him in waves. *I didn't truly*

*appreciate my life here. I could have dated anyone in this
town, but I let Dad's opinion of me become a barrier.
Worse, I have an obscene amount of money at my disposal,
and I've ignored it. Too afraid to touch it. What am I prov-
ing by letting it sit there? That Dad was right and money
is everything? It's just money. Help me let go of this fear
and resentment.*

A sense of peace washed over him. He didn't have to
keep putting limits on his life because of his father anymore.

But what about Bridget? He'd blown it with her. She
was so much more than he deserved.

He loved her. He might have fallen in love with her the
day in the coffee shop when she told him to keep his discount. She saw him for who he was.

Bridget listened to him. She accepted him.

Mac had been wrong. So fearful and stubborn and
wrong.

So what was he going to do about it?

He reached for his cell phone and scrolled to a Bible
app. The first verse hit him square in the chest. Philippians 2:4: "Look not every man on his own things, but every
man also on the things of others."

He sat back and curved his lips upward. *Okay, God,
point taken.*

It was time to deal with the donation requests. And tomorrow, he'd make things right with Bridget.

Bridget awoke with a start. Her heart was pounding
and a fine sheen of sweat glistened along her hairline.
Bad dreams. She sat up, hugging her knees to her chest
under the covers. The window revealed the break of dawn.
Snow was falling.

Christmas Eve. In Sunrise Bend.

How could she ever live here now?

She'd gotten close to Kaylee, fallen in love with Mac. They'd want nothing to do with her after last night's revelations. Tossing the covers, she got out of bed.

She'd just have to avoid them.

In this tiny town? Yeah, right.

She made her way to the kitchen to brew an espresso. Every morning—good, bad, ordinary or catastrophic—demanded coffee. As the machine fired up, she sat at the table, propped her elbows on it and let her chin rest on her fists.

What if Mac tried to end her lease early? Evict her?

Her head swam. She'd lose her apartment. Be out on the streets with her boxes and belongings. With nowhere to go.

The bad scenarios piled onto each other. She closed her eyes and covered her face with her hands. Why was her chest so tight? Was she having a heart attack?

You have a car now.

That's right. She wasn't helpless or homeless or without resources. She had a car and a driver's license. Money in the bank. Sawyer and Tess to go to. Joe would help her out in a heartbeat.

The tightness in her chest eased.

Bridget wasn't even close to being as helpless as she was at sixteen. So why did her mind sprint there?

She made a cappuccino and carried it over to the couch. Did Mac hate her? Was he embarrassed by her?

She took a sip. Too hot. She set the mug on a coaster. Her fingers automatically went to her necklace. But it wasn't there. Sheer panic zipped through her core.

Bridget raced to her bedroom and exhaled in relief when she spotted it on the bedside table. She carefully picked it up and clasped it around her neck.

Why am I so afraid? The Bible says I'm worth more than many sparrows.

. Jesus loved her so much He died for her.

Do you think He sees you as anything but worthy?

Tears sprang to her eyes.

"I'm not worthy, though." The sound of her own voice startled her.

Yes, I am. God doesn't lie. He washed away my sins for good.

Then why did she feel so unworthy? Of having a normal life, a successful coffee shop, good friends? Of Mac?

Lord, I feel so helpless. Like I want to curl into the fetal position and not leave this apartment for five days. I don't want to see anyone, especially Mac.

It would be better to be invisible.

When she'd been homeless, she'd tried to make herself invisible. She'd been so ashamed, so scared, so hungry, so dirty.

I don't need to be invisible ever again, do I?

A sense of calm stole over her.

She couldn't change her past. Yes, she'd been homeless and hungry and scared and stinky. But she wasn't anymore. By God's grace, she'd carved out a life for herself right here in Sunrise Bend.

She had nothing to be ashamed of. She didn't need to hide her past or modify her personality. God loved her. Christmas Eve was for celebrating the fact He'd sent His Son to save her. Her! Homeless, worthless her.

He'd given her a home, given her a business, given her friends, given her a sense of worth.

She was going to be all right. No matter what.

Chapter Fourteen

The next morning, Christmas Eve, Mac set his phone on the desk in the den and placed both hands behind his head. He hadn't felt this alive in years.

All those donation requests? Done. They'd been the easy tasks.

Funny, how two days ago the *easy tasks* had seemed impossible. All it had taken was one perfectly timed Bible passage to get him moving.

He'd called Dina Jones first. She'd shrieked—actually shrieked—when he told her he was donating enough to replace the uniforms for every sport *and* renovating the football stadium. She didn't strike him as overly emotional, but he'd heard the tearful joy in her thank-yous.

Next he'd contacted John Lutz and assured him he'd pay for the entire irrigation diversion project. John, shocked, had assured him it wasn't necessary, that they could do fundraisers for part of the money, but Mac had insisted. John excitedly pronounced Mary would be bringing over a double batch of cinnamon rolls later.

Mac hadn't objected. He loved her cinnamon rolls.

Then he'd gone down the line and called every person in Sunrise Bend who had requested a donation and told them he was cutting a check for a thousand dollars to their cause. And he'd told them it was courtesy of his dad, Roger Tolbert.

Donating in honor of his father felt right. More than right.

On top of that, he'd realized he didn't want to deal with a flood of requests for money every year, so next week he was calling his team of lawyers to set up a foundation for Sunrise Bend residents. If they had a need, they could apply for funds through the foundation instead of asking him.

Finally, he'd taken Bridget's advice and taken action on the one cause closest to his heart. He'd just gotten off the phone with Dr. David Carr. David mentioned the possibility of starting a satellite cancer clinic here in town. If two or three other nearby towns wanted to share costs, they could hire a small group of oncologists who would rotate between the clinics in each town and offer telehealth visits in between.

Mac would gladly fund that project.

He rose and peered out the window. It was just after 10 a.m. The snow was falling gently. Half an hour ago Kaylee had eaten a bowl of cereal and retreated to her bedroom. He hadn't had the heart to ask her about singing tonight.

His mind went back to yesterday. How he'd lost his temper. How Bridget had stood there so vulnerable as she poured her heart out to him. How she'd told him she was trash.

She wasn't trash. She was his treasure.

He couldn't imagine how painful life must have been for her after her father died. No wonder she'd never wanted to discuss it.

Bridget was brave.

And he wasn't.

The last time he'd been brave was when he'd stood up to his dad and asked to move to Sunrise Bend. That had been many years ago. What had happened to him?

It was time for him to be brave, too. Time to once more pursue the life he wanted. Bridget was the woman for him. He didn't have to worry about her walking all over him. She wasn't the type. He just prayed she'd forgive him.

It was strange how she could be pleasant to customers even while her heart was pulverized. Bridget had been selling coffee all morning as people rushed around for last-minute gifts. Brewed Awakening would be open for a few more minutes, until noon. Tomorrow, Christmas Day, the shop would be closed.

She rang out another customer and was thankful to see people leaving. As soon as the place was empty, she glided over to the front door and turned the sign from Open to Closed.

A man appeared in the doorway. She jumped back, placing her hand against her chest.

Mac pointed to the door and mouthed, *Can I come in?*

Her heart was thumping as she opened it for him. He came inside, and she locked it behind him.

Stamping his feet free from snow, he took off his gloves and gave the place a quick once-over. "Everyone went home?"

Nodding, she spun on her heel and went back to the counter where she continued emptying the dishwasher with shaking fingers. Why was he here? What was he going to say?

She looked up then and realized he'd followed her. He plucked the mug out of her hand, set it on the counter, took both her hands in his and looked deep into her eyes.

"I'm sorry for yesterday." His throat worked. "I attacked

you and it was unforgivable. I'm ashamed of the things I said, the things I accused you of. I would tell you I don't know what came over me, but I'd be lying. I know. And it had nothing to do with you."

Bridget's eyelashes fluttered. What was he talking about?

"You were honest with me about your past, and I can't tell you how sorry I am that you went through all that. I'm also sorry I didn't say all this yesterday. But since you told me what happened to you, it's only fair I tell you the truth about me, too."

The truth about him? What did he mean? Her fingers trembled, and he squeezed them.

"What you see isn't what you get with me, either." His jaw shifted. "Most people around here see me as a good guy. A rancher. Someone born wealthy. Nothing more. Honestly, they might not even see me as that. I don't know."

Bridget immediately wondered if it was true. His friends saw him as more than that, for sure, but the other people in town? He was well-liked around here. Not one person had said a word against him since she'd opened the coffee shop.

"My dad wasn't around much when I was a kid. He liked to lay down the law, though, when it came to his rules. I was pretty much raised by a rotation of nannies until I moved here as a teen. Convincing him to let me was the hard part. He wasn't having it. I wore him down, but it cost me."

"What did it cost you?" she asked quietly.

"He told me hard work would do me good but I'd better not forget the fact everyone around town knew I had money."

"As if they wouldn't like you for yourself?" What an awful thing to say to a kid.

"He also told me women would walk all over me. Last

night I realized women have never walked all over me. He did. Dad was the one who walked all over me my entire life. I can't remember a single year of ranching where he didn't threaten to take it away from me—sell it, put someone else in charge, whatever—if I didn't do things exactly the way he wanted. And I put up with it."

Just the thought of losing Brewed Awakening and her apartment had made her an anxiety-ridden wreck this morning. She couldn't imagine constantly worrying about having his ranch snatched away.

Mac let go of her hands. "I couldn't face losing the ranch. But all those compromises…all the years of going along with his demands…they wore me down. I wouldn't let a woman in, mainly because I was afraid Dad was right. She'd walk all over me, the same as he was doing. I didn't see it for what it was, though, until last night."

Bridget wanted to comfort him, but she wasn't sure how.

"Ever since Kaylee moved here, I've been a mess. You're right—I've been a pushover when it came to her, and it wasn't helping her. On top of that, getting the inheritance…" He shook his head, averting his gaze. "Every time someone wanted a donation, it was a big, fat reminder Dad had prioritized money over me my entire life. I hated it. Hated that he cared more about making a profit than spending time with me."

She suddenly understood Mac in a way she hadn't before.

He drew his shoulders back. "So I'm standing here asking you to forgive me. The real me. The wimp who wouldn't stand up to his father. The pushover who couldn't see his sister needed him to have some faith in her, not an easy way out. The jerk who accused *you* of being the problem. I'm the problem, Bridget. Me." He jabbed his thumb into his chest. "You told me you loved me. Well, I love you, too. I started loving you the minute you told me to keep my discount when I asked you to hire Kaylee. I just didn't know it. I don't blame you if your feelings have changed. I'm not the man you thought I was. But I'll be the man you need if you'll let me."

Tears stung her eyes, but they weren't tears of sadness. She was stunned and grateful and...she understood.

"You're right," she said. "You aren't the man I thought you were."

Mac's heart dropped with a thud. He'd known he was taking a risk telling her the truth.

"You're better than the man I thought you were." Bridget stepped closer, caressing his cheek. Her brown eyes shimmered with appreciation. "It's easy to look at someone like you and assume your life is perfect. I did. I won't deny it. You're so handsome and nice. It's also easy to think that because you have money, you don't have the same problems I have."

It was true. His problems were minor compared to hers growing up.

"But your problems are hard, too, Mac, and I don't want you to think they aren't. Thank you for sharing that about your father. I had no idea, and I'm sorry he didn't value you. My own father was absent in my life, too, and he looked the other way when my stepmother mistreated me. I blame him for not protecting me."

"Is that why you took such an interest in Kaylee?" he asked.

"Partly. I saw a lot of myself in her. An orphan, quiet and shy, feeling like she doesn't belong. I've dealt with the same things for most of my life. I wanted her teen years to be better than mine were. So I tried to support her as best I could, but you were right. I shouldn't have pushed her yesterday. I'm sorry for that."

"Don't be sorry. Don't ever be sorry for caring about Kaylee." He brushed her hair behind her ear. "You were right to encourage her to honor her commitments. I should have, too."

"But she was so upset." Bridget's lashes lowered. "I feel terrible."

"She's not upset at you. She told me the closer it gets to Christmas, the more she misses her mom. That's why she was upset."

"I should have known…"

"I should have, too."

Silence stretched between them.

"Bridget?"

"Hmm?"

"Where do we stand?" He needed her. He needed this woman who helped him make sense of life. He needed to hear she still loved him, that he hadn't ruined everything. "You and me? I love you. And I know there's a good chance you no longer feel the same. I wouldn't blame you."

A soft smile spread across her face, and she wrapped her arms around his neck, looking up into his eyes. "I love you, too. I'm glad we're being honest. We know the ugly stuff now, and I love you all the more for it."

The words filled him with hope and joy.

"You're no pushover," she said. "And I don't think anyone would ever walk all over you. Your father mistook your kind nature and generosity for something negative. Don't ever lose that part of you. Those are your greatest traits."

He slid his arms around her waist and kissed her. He wanted to show how much he appreciated her honesty, how much he loved her bluntness, how much he admired her integrity. He poured his heart into the kiss. And, as she kissed him back, rational thoughts fled, replaced by visions of a wedding and life together.

His city girl.

She broke away, wide-eyed and short of breath. "Oh, wow."

"Yeah." He couldn't help but grin as she fanned herself.

"Do you have any idea how much I admire you?" he asked, pressing his forehead to hers.

"No?"

"Well, I do. Not just for overcoming your past. And for the record, you are not trash. You are my treasure. I admire how you treat people and how you listen to them. I especially admire how you value Joe. A lot of people around here take him for granted, and I can see the difference you've made in his life."

"He's made a difference in mine, too." Her eyes sparkled. "He's a good friend. I'm thankful for him."

"I know." He held her waist lightly. Her perfume was doing something funny to his brain. "You know how I've been putting off all those requests for donations?"

"Yes."

"I took care of it."

"How?" She frowned slightly.

"I honored them all. Every one of them." He couldn't help but grin. It felt good to help his community. This was his home. These were his people. "I can afford it."

"And here I was certain you were going to donate to cancer research." She let her hands slide down from the back of his neck to rest against his chest.

"Oh, I'm taking on cancer, too. Hannah's brother and I are figuring out what it will take to set up a satellite clinic specifically for cancer patients here. If the neighboring towns are interested, we could have a group of oncologists taking appointments in each town on a rotating basis."

"What a great idea!" She beamed. "Tess will be thrilled."

"Ken, too."

"And Sawyer." Her face lit brighter than he thought possible. "You're a good man, Mac. I love you."

"I love you, too, Bridget." He gazed into her eyes, ready to kiss her again.

"What about Kaylee?" She frowned. "Is she singing tonight?"

"I don't know." He shook his head. "I have an idea, though."

"What is it?"

"Well, it's…" He cringed. Should he suggest it? Was it stupid? "You and I know the song inside and out. We've practiced with Kaylee for weeks."

A cloud covered her expression as her throat worked.

"And I was thinking maybe instead of a solo, the three of us could sing it." He watched her carefully.

"The three of us?" She stepped back, her eyes wide.

"Yes. You have the alto part down. I'm good on tenor. Do you think Kaylee would go for it?"

"I don't know. Maybe it should be a duet—just you and her."

It was on the tip of his tongue to tell her that was fine if it was what she wanted. However, something gave him the impression she wanted to sing but was afraid to. The same thing Kaylee had been doing for weeks.

This time, he was going to be the one to push. He'd be honest with her. He owed her that much.

"You're a part of Sunrise Bend now." He took her hand in his and kissed the back of it. "I think you should sing with us. I think people would enjoy seeing this part of you."

"You do?"

"Yeah, I do." He couldn't pinpoint why, exactly, but he

knew it had something to do with how ashamed she was of her past.

"Maybe you're right. When I moved here, I told myself to keep a low profile, to not reveal too much. I was worried I'd be rejected."

Judging from the worry pursing her lips, he'd say this was the first time she'd ever even considered doing something that would put her in the spotlight.

"You won't be rejected. You have a lot of people here who care about you."

"I think you're right." She began to nod, clearly overwhelmed but working through it. "If Kaylee agrees, I'll do it."

"Come on." He offered her his arm. "Let's go back to the ranch and ask her together."

"You're sure about this?" She took his arm.

"I'm sure."

He'd never been so sure of anything in his life.

Chapter Fifteen

"I don't know if I can do it," Kaylee said.

Bridget kept her mouth shut, disappointed that Kaylee wasn't jumping at the chance of singing with them. Mac squeezed Bridget's knee where she sat next to him on the sectional in his family room. Kaylee had stretched her legs out on the attached chaise longue.

They'd arrived a few minutes ago, and after waiting for Kaylee to change out of her pajamas, Mac had told her they were dating. Her reaction had made Bridget's day. Kaylee had hugged them both, declaring this was the best Christmas gift she could have imagined. Then Mac had mentioned his idea about the three of them singing the solo, and the girl had shrunk into herself like old times.

"Would you be willing to try?" Mac asked gently. "If the three of us were up there and you felt like you were going to lose it, you could stop singing."

"Mac and I could sing the rest." Bridget gave her a tender smile.

"Why don't you two sing it? I'll just watch." Kaylee was picking imaginary lint off her leggings.

"You could do that," Bridget said. "But I remember how happy you were the day you told me you'd joined the

Christmas choir. And I know how special it was for you to sing with your mom every year. That's why you signed up."

Kaylee looked up. "I didn't think I'd be so sad. I didn't think I'd miss her so much."

"I know," Mac said. "It seems to me like singing is a way to keep her memory close to you."

"I do feel better today." Fear lingered in her eyes. "But I don't know if I can make it through the song without crying. I don't know if it's the song that triggers it or what."

"That's fair." Mac nodded.

"You guys would really sing with me?" Kaylee asked.

"Yeah," Mac said. "We want to."

"Absolutely," Bridget said.

Kaylee tilted her chin up. "Okay. I'm in. I think Mom would want me to keep the tradition going. She wouldn't want me to quit. Not on Christmas Eve."

Bridget was amazed at the light in her face. She was always pretty, and right now she glowed.

"I'll call the choir director and let her know there's been a slight change in plans." Mac pushed off the couch to stand, bent to kiss Bridget's cheek then grinned and left the room.

Kaylee came over to sit by her.

"Did Mac tell you I overheard you guys talking yesterday?"

"He didn't." Bridget's stomach soured instantly.

"I'm sorry all that happened to you, Bridget." Her eyes gleamed with sympathy. "Everything was taken away from you. And you're not bitter. You don't hide from your problems. I want to be more like you."

The words wrapped around her heart like a hug.

"I did hide, though, Kaylee." Bridget had to be honest with her. "Maybe not in body, but in spirit. I've been afraid of being myself because it felt like I had a target on my back. Remember the day you stood up for Joe when Janet made a fuss?"

She nodded.

"I knew right then and there I had to stop hiding in spirit. I was ashamed of myself. I had to start sticking up for my friends, for my beliefs, and that was because of you."

"You? You always stick up for me. You're one of the few people who gets me at all."

"Well, I guess we're a good pair." She put her arm around Kaylee's shoulders. "We make each other want to be better."

Kaylee gave her a side hug. "I'm glad you're dating Mac. I think you guys should get married."

"It's a little soon for that." But Bridget loved the idea of forever with him.

"I'd better start getting ready." Kaylee scooched off the couch. "If I'm doing this, I'm going to look good."

"You always look good."

Mac returned as Kaylee headed to her room. He jerked his thumb in her direction as he approached Bridget. "Is she okay?"

"Yep. Getting ready for tonight."

"This early?" He lowered his frame next to her, his thigh pressing against hers as he slung his arm over her shoulders.

"It's only a few hours from now."

"A few hours?" He gave her a sly glance. "Plenty of time."

"For what?" she asked innocently.

"For this." He lowered his mouth to hers.

Yep. They had plenty of time. She sank into his embrace. Plenty.

"I don't think I can do this," Bridget whispered.

Mac studied her face. She looked pale and nervous.

Kaylee, sitting on the other side of her in the pew, patted Bridget's hand. "You can. I'm right here next to you."

And here he'd thought he and Bridget would have to be
giving Kaylee the pep talk. Nope. Bridget was the nervous
wreck. Kaylee, to her credit, seemed serene.

"Kaylee's right," he whispered. "You're going to be
great."

He leaned forward and caught Kaylee's eye. She gave
him a thumbs-up.

The pastor wrapped up the reading from Luke chapter
two. This was their cue.

Mac stood and waited for Bridget and Kaylee to exit
the pew before following them up to the microphone. Kaylee stood in the middle, he stood to her left, and Bridget
stood to her right.

The pianist began playing "To Shepherds as They
Watched by Night," and Mac was filled with Christmas
joy. *Lord, thank You for these two women who have become my entire life in just a few short months. Please give
Bridget and Kaylee the courage to sing.*

And then it was time. Kaylee's voice projected clearly,
purely, and Mac joined in, relieved to hear Bridget's
voice—wobbly at first—gaining strength. The first verse
ended and the second began. As they continued, the three
of them blended in harmony, filling the church with the
love of Christ. When it ended, they quietly made their
way back to their seats, where Mac held Bridget's hand.

"I'm proud of you," he whispered. With tears in her
eyes, she squeezed his hand. "Both of you," he added,
smiling at Kaylee. The rest of the service went by in the
blink of an eye, and soon they were mingling with everyone in the narthex.

Dina Jones practically sprinted to Mac, gushing at his
generosity. Bridget edged away, but he caught her hand and

wouldn't let go. Then another person took Dina's place. On and on it went with thank-yous and hugs for helping with the pavilion and the hospital bills and…he just smiled and listened and wished them all a merry Christmas.

During a lull, Bridget leaned into his ear. "Look at all the Christmas wishes you made come true. You're a good man."

He slipped his arm around her waist. "It wasn't me. This is all God. These people are my community. I want to help them, because even if they don't know it, they all helped me by giving me a place where I feel at home."

"I know what you mean." Her gorgeous black, slim-fitting dress—simple and elegant, the same as her—took his breath away for the thousandth time that night. He chided himself to focus on what she was saying. "Every person who comes into my shop is part of my community. They made it possible for me to make my home here."

"I'm glad you made your home here."

"I am, too."

Kaylee rushed over, and to Mac's surprise, Tanner was right behind her. "Mac, I want you to meet Tanner Voss. Tanner, this is my brother, Mac."

Mac nodded, shaking the kid's hand. "Good to meet you."

"You, too, sir." Tanner maintained eye contact with him, which was a point in his favor. "I wanted to thank you, too, for helping out the school. My best friend, Dante, plays football, and he's pumped about the uniforms. The new football stadium is going to be awesome, too."

"Do you go to the games?" Mac asked, not loathing the kid as much as he thought he would.

"Yeah, when I can. I'm on the rodeo team. Horses are in my blood."

His kind of guy. "Mine, too. You should come over

sometime." Mac glanced at Kaylee, who seemed beside herself with happiness. "Kaylee and you could ride. I've got a lot of land."

"I'd like that."

Mac's friends came up to them. Austin carried baby AJ, Randy and Hannah held hands, Jet and Holly kept a firm grip on Clara as she walked between them and Blaine was with his sister Reagan. Tess, Sawyer and little Tucker trailed the group.

Sawyer eyed the way Mac was holding Bridget's hand before giving her a hug. "I think we have a lot of catching up to do."

"What do you mean?" Bridget played coy.

Mac slid his arm around her waist and grinned. "He means he wants to know if we're dating."

The group went silent with excited anticipation.

Mac held perfectly still, waiting to see how Bridget would respond.

"Well, then, I guess we should tell them." She looked into his eyes, hers dancing with merriment.

"We're dating." He loved the sound of it. Loved saying it out loud.

After everyone congratulated them, they found their coats and made their way out to the parking lot with Kaylee. When they got into the truck and Mac started heading home, Bridget turned to the back seat.

"So, what's going on with you and Tanner?"

Mac listened attentively.

"He asked me out. It's a group thing, Mac, so don't get all big brothery on me. A bunch of us are riding the trails next week."

"On horses or four-wheelers?" Mac asked. He liked the idea of a group thing. And he liked the idea of Kaylee enjoying the beauty of Wyoming in the winter with her friends.

"If the weather's nice, horses. If it's not nice, we're watching movies at Kendra's house."

Bridget clapped. "I knew he liked you. Did he kiss you yet?"

"Bridget!" Kaylee yelled. "Mac's here. Eww."

"Point taken." She faced the front. "You sang beautifully, Kaylee. I know your mom would have been proud. I sure was. But, boy, I thought I was going to pass out before the first stanza started. My voice was so tinny. Did you hear it? Yikes…"

Mac turned on the radio and they sang Christmas songs all the way home. As soon as they got inside, Kaylee ran to her room, claiming she had to tell Lydia everything, while he and Bridget went to the family room. He flipped the switch on the gas fireplace and turned on the Christmas tree lights. Then he picked up a small gift bag from under the tree and joined Bridget where she stood by the windows, staring out into the night.

"You're beautiful." He kissed her cheek lightly, and she turned, smiling up at him. "I have a gift for you."

"You do?"

He nodded, handing her the gold bag with silver frills. She took it shyly as if she wasn't sure what to do.

"It's not going to open itself," he teased, drinking in her stunning face.

Her lips twitched, and she pulled the wrapped box from the bag. Then she tore off the paper and lifted the lid.

She gasped. "Sparrows? Really?"

The sparrow earrings perfectly matched her necklace. He'd searched far and wide for them. He touched the sparrow in the hollow of her throat. "I've never seen you without the necklace."

"I bought it when I got baptized on my twentieth birthday." Her soft smile made her even more beautiful. "There's a passage in the Bible that says you are worth more than many sparrows. It reminds me of how God plucked me off the streets and gave me a home, even before I believed in Him. That's how good He is."

Mac couldn't agree more. "When I think of all my blessings, I'm humbled. You're right, Bridget. God is good."

"I love you, Mac."

"I love you more than you could ever imagine."

"Merry Christmas," she said.

"You're the best Christmas gift I've ever gotten."

Epilogue

Mac's hands trembled as he strode toward Brewed Awakening on Valentine's Day. Two dozen pink roses wrapped in kraft paper were nestled in the crook of his arm. It was a Monday afternoon, and he was there under the pretense of picking Kaylee up from work. She'd gotten her driver's license a week after her birthday, but a winter storm had shut everything down for days, and they'd both agreed she should wait until the weather improved to drive by herself. None of that mattered at the moment.

He was ready to propose to Bridget. What if she turned him down?

Peering through the front window, he smiled as he watched Bridget laugh at something Kaylee said. Then Joe came through the doorway from the back room and motioned for Bridget to come back there.

That was Mac's cue.

As soon as Bridget went to the back room, Mac hurried inside, and Kaylee began setting the table up front. When she finished with the drinks and dessert, she ran up to him with sparkling eyes. "Did you get it? Are you ready?"

"Got it. Ready." He patted his pants pocket for the ring. Yep. Still there.

"Okay, I have everything else all set. Joe and I will go to the Barking Squirrel for thirty minutes. Not one minute longer, though!" She hugged him, took the flowers and shoved them behind the counter, then practically sprinted to the back.

Muffled voices distracted him for a moment. He'd mentally rehearsed this moment no less than five hundred times. The guys had *tried* to help this weekend, but his friends were simply not good at proposal ideas.

Randy was still on his fishing-pole-and-reeling-her-in idea, even though the man had personally proposed in a non-moronic way to Hannah. Blaine told him to throw the ring in a jar of coffee beans and have her find it. Dumb. Then Jet had mentioned taking her on a horseback ride, which wouldn't have been bad except for the fact Bridget had never been on a horse and the temperature outside was in the teens. Even Sawyer, who should have known better, had told him to just ask her. To keep it simple.

This was Bridget. She deserved better than simple.

Why did his throat feel scratchy all of a sudden?

"Well, hello, handsome." Bridget beamed when she saw him. "Kaylee should be right out."

He went straight to her and kissed her cheek. The music from the speakers switched to romantic songs from yesteryear. The lights dimmed. Then Joe and Kaylee came out of the back room, waving to them both. "We'll be back in a bit."

Bridget squinted, wrinkling her nose. "Where are they going? That's weird. They didn't say anything to me. And Kaylee didn't even clear the front table. What is going on with her? The chocolates Tanner brought by must have messed with her head."

She let out a huff and took a step forward, but Mac stopped her. He took her by the hand and led her to the table. Strands of white lights twinkled overhead. Two mugs of cappuccino with hearts drawn in the steamed milk sat there with an elegant chocolate torte in the middle of the table.

"Ooh, is this a Valentine's Day thing?" Her eyes shimmered as he pulled out a chair for her.

"Yes." He went behind the counter and brought out the flowers, handing them to her. She promptly brought them up to her nose and inhaled their sweet aroma before setting them on the table. "It's a Valentine's Day thing. And…" His palms were sweaty, his mouth as dry as day-old toast. The fancy speech he'd planned flew out of his mind.

"And?" She looked puzzled.

"And more."

There. He could do this.

He blinked twice and gulped. "Bridget, my love, you are everything I could want in a woman and more. Much more than I deserve. This is going to sound dumb, but your simple style does something to me. And sometimes I come in just to watch you make lattes. There's a precision to what you do that I find mesmerizing."

"You think me making a latte is mesmerizing?" Her lashes fluttered as she watched him.

"Yeah, I do. In fact, everything about you captivates me. The way you laugh. The way you know someone's having a rough time but you sit there and listen and always have the right thing to say to make them feel better. I even like the way you drive, but then, I'm probably biased since I taught you."

Her lips twitched with laughter.

"I guess what I'm saying is you're the cream to my coffee, the espresso to my latte. I love you." He got down on one knee and pulled out the black box. Almost dropped it as he fumbled to open it. "Bridget Renna, will you marry me?"

Tears dropped one by one to her cheeks as her hands clasped over her chest. She was nodding and smiling, though, so he took that as a good thing.

"Yes, oh Mac, yes!"

He rose, pulling her up with him, and hugged her tightly until she placed her hands on his cheeks and stood on her tiptoes to kiss him.

He tasted coffee, love and forever in her kiss.

"You mean it? You'll really marry me?" he asked huskily, keeping her close.

"Yes." She grinned. "I'll marry you. When?"

"Tomorrow?" He held her by the waist.

"That might be too soon." She slid her arms around his neck and tilted her head to gaze into his eyes. "How about later this summer? I've always had a thing for September."

"September it is, then."

"We were meant for each other, Mac."

"I couldn't agree more."

* * * * *

*If you enjoyed this Wyoming Ranchers story
by Jill Kemerer, be sure to pick up
the previous books in the series:*

The Prodigal's Holiday Hope
A Cowboy to Rely On
Guarding His Secret

Available now from Love Inspired!

Dear Reader,

Merry Christmas to you! I couldn't wait to tell Mac's story, because he needed a woman who saw right through to the heart of him. Bridget viewed him as more than a nice, wealthy rancher. She saw what a kind, generous man he really was, not the pushover his dad had predicted.

The idea for this book came to me when I was sitting in a coffee shop one day. I watched the interaction between the employees and the customers, and I started thinking about an owner who had a special way with people, but who also had secrets she didn't want revealed.

We all have things in our past we're ashamed of. They might be big, like Bridget's being homeless, or they might be internal, like Mac's feelings about his father. The important thing is to not let them keep us from living a full life. Like Bridget, we can take comfort in the fact that when we feel insignificant, God does not view us that way at all. As it says in Matthew 10:31, "Fear ye not therefore, ye are of more value than many sparrows."

Let us overflow with hope by the power of the Holy Spirit, no matter what comes our way. I hope you enjoyed this book. I love connecting with readers. Feel free to email me at jill@jillkemerer.com or write me at P.O. Box 2802, Whitehouse, Ohio, 43571.

Have a blessed Christmas season!
Jill Kemerer

**WE HOPE YOU ENJOYED
THIS BOOK FROM**

LOVE INSPIRED
INSPIRATIONAL ROMANCE

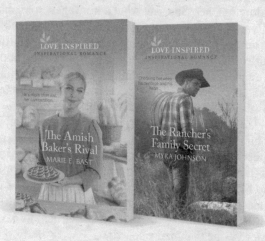

Uplifting stories of faith, forgiveness and hope.

Fall in love with stories where faith helps
guide you through life's challenges, and discover
the promise of a new beginning.

6 NEW BOOKS AVAILABLE EVERY MONTH!

HARLEQUIN
PLUS

Announcing a **BRAND-NEW** multimedia subscription service for romance fans like you!

Read, Watch and Play.

Experience the easiest way to get the romance content you crave.

Start your **FREE 7 DAY TRIAL** at
<u>www.harlequinplus.com/freetrial</u>.

SPECIAL EXCERPT FROM

LOVE INSPIRED
INSPIRATIONAL ROMANCE

When a service dog brings them together,
will secrets tear them apart?

Read on for a sneak preview of
An Alaskan Christmas Promise
by Belle Calhoune.

Kit O'Malley gripped the steering wheel tightly as she navigated down the snow-covered Alaskan roads. Her recent medical diagnosis had turned her life upside down, and now all she could think about was losing her eyesight. Kit didn't believe anything could ever fully prepare a person for such a blow.

She'd confided her diagnosis to her sister, who'd told her about Leo Duggan's work with service dogs. Jules had encouraged her to seek out Leo to see if she could adopt one of his canines. Ever since, Kit had been holding on to the idea like a lifeline.

She had never considered herself to be particularly brave, but over the past few weeks she'd been feeling extremely vulnerable and weak. At the moment she needed to focus on the matter at hand—beseeching Leo to consider her request.

As she approached the Duggan Ranch, Kit drove up to a gate emblazoned with a big *D* on it. Up ahead Kit